## *"What's gotten into you.* he as...

I drive you back from Titus Canyon and you're a tomb the whole trip, then you suddenly bite my head off for who knows what reason. I swear, Claire. I can't make heads or tails out of you."

"Me?" she said shrilly. "I'm the tomb? That's terrific coming from you."

Suddenly the tension sparkled between them again, and if Claire had paused, she would have known she was on dangerous ground.

"You're the one with all the secrets," she continued. "I don't even know what you're doing in Death Valley. Even when you do start to say something, you clam up. It's as if you don't trust yourself. And then touching me the way you did this afternoon...."

Raleigh stood quietly, his face cold and closed. Only his eyes seemed alive, and they examined her with a tight fury. "Clearly I should have given you a dossier with all my personal information before I offered to drive you around. Unfortunately I didn't."

In three strides he was in his car, and Claire was still scowling at him, cursing his dust as he pulled away. *Damn the man.*

Dear Reader,

Although our culture is always changing, the desire to love and be loved is a constant in every woman's heart. Silhouette Romances reflect that desire, sweeping you away with books that will make you laugh and cry, poignant stories that will move you time and time again.

This year we're featuring Romances with a playful twist. Remember those fun-loving heroines who always manage to get themselves into tricky predicaments? You'll enjoy reading about their escapades in Silhouette Romances by Brittany Young, Debbie Macomber, Annette Broadrick and Rita Rainville.

We're also publishing Romances by many of your all-time favorites such as Ginna Gray, Diana Palmer and Joan Hohl. Your overwhelming reaction to these authors has served as a touchstone for us, and we're pleased to bring you more books with Silhouette's distinctive medley of charm, wit and—above all—*romance*. I hope you enjoy this book, and the many stories to come.

Sincerely,

Rosalind Noonan
Senior Editor
SILHOUETTE BOOKS

# MARY O'CARAGH
## Mirage

*Silhouette* *Romance*

Published by Silhouette Books New York

**America's Publisher of Contemporary Romance**

For the S.O.N. Club

SILHOUETTE BOOKS
300 E. 42nd St., New York, N.Y. 10017

Copyright © 1986 by Mary O'Caragh

ISBN: 0-373-08445-5

First Silhouette Books printing July 1986

America's Publisher of Contemporary Romance

Printed in the U.S.A.

### *MARY O'CARAGH*

has been an avid reader ever since she discovered the backs of cereal boxes. She began writing seriously two years ago, and quickly found that it was the perfect occupation for her, as it draws on her other interests, including travel, art, music, science, romance and, most of all, people. Mary grew up in St. Paul, Minnesota, as the fourth of seven brothers and sisters. "And that was an adventure in itself!"

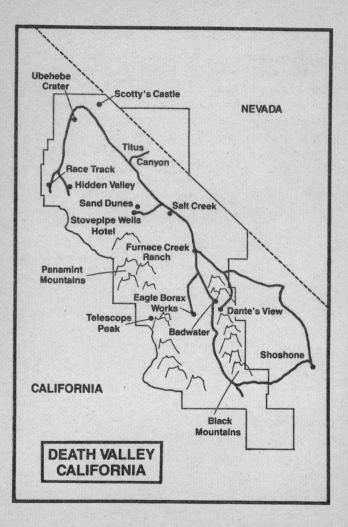

Ubehebe
Crater

Scotty's Castle

NEVADA

Titus
Canyon

Race Track
Hidden Valley

Sand Dunes

Salt Creek

Stovepipe Wells
Hotel

Furnace Creek
Ranch

Panamint
Mountains

Eagle Borax
Works

Dante's View

Telescope
Peak

Badwater

Shoshone

CALIFORNIA

Black
Mountains

**DEATH VALLEY
CALIFORNIA**

# Chapter One

Gripping the wheel tightly to convince herself she was still awake, Claire Bennett steered her Scout around the base of the cliff and stepped on the accelerator. During her three months in Death Valley, she had come to know its few highways so well she could see every curve in her sleep. It was a good thing, too, she thought, considering how tired she was. Towering above her, the clay cliffs shone a dull red where the evening sun still reached them, and on her left, the salt flats were reduced to a maze of shadows. It was distractingly lovely. She looked back at the road and swerved sharply, just in time to avoid a car that had pulled up on the shoulder.

She quickly pulled over and backed up until she was just in front of the other car. She knew it was dangerous to be stranded in the desert at night, and she leaned far out the window, looking for the driver.

"Hey," she called. Her voice was low, but it carried in the stillness. "Do you need any help?" She waited. "Is anybody there?"

A large dark form straightened at the far side of the other car, and she thought she heard a curse. Claire could see now that the car was jacked up and there were tools strewn on the pavement.

"Is it a flat?" she called, beginning to wonder if the man understood English.

"No," he hollered back. "I just thought I'd change a tire for fun. Why don't you stick around and we'll try the other three."

Generally, Claire would have started her car and driven off right then and there. The man was very much in control of his situation, and he was obviously a boor. She had had an exhausting day and the last of her energy concentrated itself into severe annoyance. Who did this guy think he was talking to?

"I'd love to help," she said, "but I think I'll just watch instead. Since we don't need to worry about your safety, I've got plenty of time to waste."

He started to walk over to her car.

"What's that supposed to mean?" he asked.

"Well, at noon there's sunstroke, and at midnight there's exposure to the cold and the cutthroats." She sweetened her tone. "No doubt you could handle those just fine too, though."

He stood motionless there in the dimness. Had he understood her, or was he slow as well as rude? A couple of swift strides brought him full up to her window, and she made out a firm chin and an expression in his eyes that did not suggest stupidity.

"Probably," he agreed evenly, "but as far as safety goes, you're not much of an authority."

For the first time, Claire sensed a vague threat about the man; something in the way he carried himself. She had a temptation to turn her key in the ignition, but she resisted. It was her turn to ask what he meant.

"Look at yourself," he began slowly. "A chivalrous woman pulls up to offer help to a stranger. She turns off her car and is on the point of getting out."

He paused, letting his words have their effect.

"What would you do, I wonder," he said, gently now, but with an edge she couldn't miss. "What would you do if I suddenly opened your door and dragged you out of the car?"

Claire caught her breath.

"You wouldn't dare," she whispered.

He took a step closer, and for a full second, a thread of pure energy spun between them, leaving Claire breathless when he stepped back suddenly and laughed.

"Yes, I would dare," he said. "But why bother? You already know all about exposure and criminals, so there's probably nothing I could do to surprise you."

He was laughing at her! The audacity of it made her furious, and instantly the illusive communion she had imagined was dispelled. He stuck one hand in his pocket, and the other playfully swung a wrench he had been holding the whole time. A glimmer of white teeth came from the dark face. He had been teasing her. Suddenly she caught another meaning in his words, and felt herself blushing. She swallowed hard and hoped her color couldn't be seen in the fading light. She faced him with as much dignity as she could muster.

"I beg your pardon for disturbing you," she said primly. "Since you don't need me to alert the ranger, I'll leave." She winced at the stiffness of her own words, and started her car, finally, wondering why she had ever

pulled off. Unwittingly, she made the mistake of looking out the window once more.

The man was grinning broadly now, and waving
goodbye with his wrench.

"Thank you so very much," he said humbly, and
nearly bowed.

He turned back to his car as she sent the Scout bar-
reling down the highway. Furiously, she jerked around
the gears and drove rapidly the rest of the way to Furnace Creek. As she pulled into the parking lot with unnecessary momentum, she noticed that her fatigue had
fled.

What nerve that guy had!

She parked the Scout behind her trailer, pulled her
knapsack out of the back and carried it to the door.
After fumbling clumsily with the lock, she finally managed to get everything inside and, at the comforting sight
of her own mess, began to relax. By the time she had
distributed her gear over the table, she was herself again,
and she gave a short laugh. At least he'd had a sense of
humor.

She turned on the radio, adjusting to the station with
the least static, and then she started heating a can of
soup before heading for the shower. The hot water felt
wonderful, and it eased the final tenseness from her
shoulders and refreshed her as she hadn't thought was
possible. Just before she finished, she turned the faucet
full force to cold, then jumped out as the first blast of icy
water hit her neck. She shivered and grabbed a towel.
Her brother had once told her that this was his version
of a sauna. "Chicken Sauna" he called it.

The mirror was fogged, so she toweled her sun-
reddened hair without bothering to see how it shaped up.
She hardly dared to look at herself these days anyway;

since her arrival three months before, her short haircut had been growing madly, and she knew a spray of freckles had emerged across the bridge of her straight nose. She had never admired her particular kind of looks, wondering if she would look girlish until the end of her days. Her violet eyes were too frank for her taste. What she didn't realize was that her low, musical voice—unexpected from her piquant face—made a combination that was bewitchingly attractive, and that made an impression of childishness impossible. Working outdoors had filled out the lines of her tall, shapely figure, and the vastness of her surroundings had somehow drawn out a grace in the way she moved and carried herself. The sun had caught the red lights in her auburn hair and, if she had had a proper mirror, she would have had to acknowledge that she was far from homely. However, Claire Bennett hadn't had any time lately to be curious about her looks.

Pulling on a loose, oversize shirt and her cotton briefs, she took the soup off the stove and opened the door to catch any breeze that might pass through. With a cup of soup, crackers and half a cantaloupe, she settled herself on the one clear seat in the miniature living space and put her feet up.

Only one more week, she thought. Much as she loved the desert project that had brought her there, she would be glad to get back to a regular apartment—with a real kitchen and real neighbors restraining their dogs in the elevator; an apartment she wouldn't share with anyone else, if she could help it. Her eyes scanned the cluttered trailer. To anyone else it would look like utter chaos, but to her it was very definitely ordered. She preferred to think of it as negative entropy: the making of organization out of disorder, possible only with creation, or originality. Claire smiled to herself. Or in extreme cases, with a research project.

Half a year before, she had submitted a postdoctorate proposal to a new geology committee in San Francisco. Employees referred to it affectionately as Earthquakes Inc., and she'd found herself thinking of it that way too. Harris Dell, the supervisor who'd made the phone call when the grant was awarded, had laughed, saying her project didn't have all that much to do with earthquakes but it was the most intriguing and thoroughly thought-out proposal they'd seen. He added as an afterthought that it was also the least expensive. Claire had thanked her lucky stars for some penny-pinching soul, and decided that she was flattered and honored.

At the time, she'd been living at home and finishing her studies at the University of Chicago, and the grant looked like the opportunity of a lifetime. A good recommendation would launch her career, opening doors to universities across the country.

Her uncle had been skeptical. "You're just like your parents," he'd said, as if that settled it.

Claire couldn't disagree. Her parents were nothing but a far-off memory, for they had been killed in a boating accident when she was only twelve. When she thought of them at all, she remembered laughter and her father's long fingers reaching to pick her up, and a general transitoriness that came with traveling often. Claire and her elder brother, Thomas, had grown up with her aunt and uncle, and ever since Thomas had shown an irresponsible streak and moved away, they had hoped Claire would get involved with their furniture business. After all, her father had been a silent partner, and one of the junior partners had an eye out for her. It would have been per-

fect for everyone but Claire. She stubbornly stuck to her
studies despite their efforts to dissuade her, and finally
they had given up. She never told them that her determination had been resolved by the young man himself.
She had discovered just in time that his affection for her
was based solely on her convenient connection to the
business. It had been a bitter surprise, but that was long
ago. Now she was an independent woman, on her own.
The only uncomfortable thing about the project was
Harris Dell himself. He had helped her get settled in
Furnace Creek in the first place, and during those few
days he had made it clear that his interest in her was
more than professional. She had managed to keep him
at a distance, but it had taken a great deal of tact, and
she had taken refuge in allowing him to think she might
be more appreciative of him later. It was cowardly, she
knew. She wasn't sure why she hadn't been more re-
sponsive. Harris was attractive, in that sunny Califor-
nian way, and he was certainly clever enough. There was
something about his slick self-assurance, though;
something that put her on her guard. She would have to
watch her step, because offending Harris would make
things very awkward. Perhaps next time they met she
would be able to reciprocate his feelings. But she
doubted it, and the idea inspired no enthusiasm, though
she would try to keep an open mind.

She had gotten to the end of her cantalope, and the
shell rocked gently on the tabletop. She took a slow
breath, not wanting to get up quite yet. Despite the clut-
ter, the trailer could be very empty at times. She had deliberately left it plain, not wanting to invest precious time
in so temporary a home. The darkroom had been the one
indulgence. It had taken her three weeks and the advice
of a professional to convert the back room to a tiny lab,

complete with proper drainage and ventilation. The committee had picked up that tab, too, and she had had to agree that it was a good investment. She had some exceptional photos, which would be an invaluable addition to the more documentary material. It was all very well, she supposed, but the utilitarian aspect of her "home" had begun to wear on her.

Quickly, she tidied the dishes, making mental lists of the things she wanted to add to her project until the lists got so long she had to jot a couple down. Her plans completely absorbed her as she mechanically pulled out the bed and washed up, but as she closed the door and slipped between the sheets, an image of the annoying man on the roadside intruded into her thoughts.

There had been something about him, about the tallness of his frame against the last light of the sky, and his mirth as he turned the tables on her. He was insufferably rude and yet, when he threatened her, he had belied himself with the gentleness of his voice. She realized, to her surprise, that she must have trusted him, for she could easily have locked her door at least, and she hadn't. Claire gave herself a shake. She had been working too hard again, and her mind was rebelling by launching off on a fruitless tangent. She would most likely never see him again, much less recognize him; and it was just as well. Yet, even as she thought this, she knew there was a possibility. Death Valley Monument covered a large area, but there were few developed places, and even fewer people. The ones who stayed for more than a few days were bound to see each other, as Claire had already discovered. She was oddly disturbed by the thought, and then irritated at being disturbed. No man had interrupted her work for what seemed like years now, despite various concerted efforts. She had learned the hard way about trusting a handsome face. Learned too well, her uncle would say. Be that as it may, no wrench-wielder was going to keep her away from her sleep.

The morning stillness was already promising a hot day when Claire loaded up her Scout. Just what I need, she thought. Awakening early had never been one of her fortes, and the coffee in her system was taking its time. She blinked lazily out her windshield. Although it was barely the middle of March, a windless day would be stifling in the desert, and Claire generally made a point of getting her more active business out of the way well before lunchtime. This morning she was already an hour later than she had intended, for a heavy dream had caught her just at dawn and caused her to sleep through her alarm. She had awakened in a rotten mood, and then the toaster hadn't worked and her bottle of sunscreen had slipped and shattered in the bathroom sink.

"What is wrong with me?" she had said to herself, shaking her head in exasperation as she picked up the slivers. It had taken forever just to get into the car, making sure she had everything she needed for the day: glasses, canteen, whistle, notebook, pick, hat and other equipment. So, turning the key, she'd headed for the Furnace Creek Ranch, where a small store carried the necessities. Only a couple of other people were up and stirring, and this somehow reassured her that the day was not so very old. She got the new bottle of sunscreen and waved to Jolly Avalos as she swung back into her car. Jolly was setting up her date stand, and she paused to grin and holler hello. Jolly's nickname suited her even in the early-morning bustle. The smile did wonders for

Claire. *I was just lonesome for a familiar face,* she thought.

Driving past the hotel, she glanced up at the picture windows. Weeks before, she had promised herself she would go there for a good dinner, and spend the sunset on the spacious terrace with something long and cool. She had saved the evening, looking forward to it, and she intentionally avoided the hotel so that she would enjoy discovering it all the more. She speculated about the people she would see there. Who would vacation in Death Valley? Obviously some people did, and by the looks of their cars, it wasn't because they couldn't afford to go somewhere else. As she passed the parking lot, her eyes suddenly doubled back. There, parked sedately under a tamarack tree and showing a well-tended shine she hadn't noticed in the dark, was the green Fiat Spider from the night before. So the gentleman was still in town.

Claire took an odd satisfaction in the fact, and surprised herself. You really have been alone too much, she scolded herself. She grinned inwardly. There was no harm in appreciating the sight of a nice car. She concentrated on the road and headed for Badwater.

Badwater. The name had a succinctness about it that appealed to her. A surveyor's mule had once refused to drink there. Claire parked in the tourist lot and walked down to take a token look at the salty little pool. It had been thought to be the lowest place in the Western Hemisphere until two spots out on the salt flats were found to be two feet lower. Claire settled her sunglasses on her nose and looked across the valley. She knew from her studies that bedrock was nearly eight thousand feet below the apparent structure of the valley floor, and she tried to imagine a drop between the two mountain ranges that would be even deeper than the one she could see. It was a favorite trick of hers. She walked a short distance down the trail and stopped. No sound penetrated the extreme stillness of the view; not even a breeze came to whistle in her ears. It was disturbing, but starkly beautiful, with the white salt stretching out harshly before her. For a moment she forgot everything and stood, turning slowly, absorbing the heat and the distance. Without knowing why, she had a feeling that this was the last time she would experience this savage serenity, and she fixed her eyes on it to capture it always in her memory. No place had ever had the impact on her that this grand, austere valley had.

Sobered, she went back and got her knapsack and headed for the cliffs. The morning vanished as Claire's work consumed her, and reluctantly she left Badwater for her next site.

Tule Spring and the Eagle Borax Works ruins were down the West Side Road, which was rough and seldom used by tourists. The Scout rattled along, and Claire shook with the steering wheel as she barreled over yet another irregular pit. This rugged traveling seemed to be the story of her life, but she had to admit she liked it. From a distance she spotted the green that heralded the river, and as she got closer she was surprised to see that she would not be alone. A pair of people were walking along the ruins, and it took her only a second to recognize the man from the evening before. His form and height were not to be mistaken, and as he turned to look at the sound of her car, she saw he was darkly tanned. He and his slender companion followed her to the parking lot. As the man recognized Claire, he walked forward.

"Come to rescue me again, have you?" he queried.

"Hardly," Claire replied, getting out of the car. "Though you do seem to have a knack for winding up in odd places. What brings you here?"

"I could ask you the same question," he said.

They faced each other, and she felt a whisper of a thrill, reminiscent of the night before. She was trying to think of a reply when his companion walked up beside him and gracefully slid her hand into his elbow.

"Friend of yours, Raleigh?" she asked, smiling appraisingly at Claire.

"More of an acquaintance really," he said, "but it's certainly time we met. I'm Raleigh Durban, and this is Miss Blake."

"Sophie," she corrected, as if amused, and reached lazily forward to shake hands.

"I'm Claire Bennett," she replied, turning to accept Raleigh's hand as well. "I'm finishing up a geology project here in the valley, and this is one of my sites. Have you been looking at the ruins?"

For a second, Sophie looked confused, and then Raleigh said smoothly:

"Yes, and the remains of the mesquite."

"Of course," Claire said. "I'd heard there was a fire."

She glanced around. Indeed, half the area was lush with mesquite and grasses, which stopped at an abrupt line where a rancher had accidentally set fire to some of the mesquite. The contrast reminded her of burned fields at the end of harvest—sad but intriguing—and she turned back to the couple reluctantly.

On second look, Claire decided they made a striking pair. Raleigh was taller than she had guessed the night before, and he carried himself with an ease that showed the grace and self-possession of an athlete. His black short-sleeved shirt did nothing to dim his ruddy tan, and a camera was slung over his shoulder with a familiarity unusual for a tourist. His hair was short and unequivocally black. His brows were dark too, and Claire was startled to find light-blue eyes watching her from under his thick lashes. There was something naggingly familiar about the man, but she was sure she would have remembered meeting him before.

Sophie was his counterpart, but eased and polished. Her face was flawlessly pale, with full lips lightly shaped in a discreet hue. Her dark shoulder-length hair caught the light as she turned her head, and her dark eyes were intelligent and heavy-lidded. In her slick summer outfit, she looked cool and unruffled, and Claire thought her eyes wandered around the area as if accustomed to looking for a waiter. If appearances were everything, the two of them were ideally suited. Unconsciously, Claire straightened.

Sophie was whispering to Raleigh, and he nodded. Then she turned to Claire.

"Miss Bennett, Raleigh and I are having a little party tomorrow evening. 'Dessert in the Desert,'" she said, with a self-indulgent shrug. "We've asked some friends to stop by, and one of them who works at the planetarium has volunteered to show us some stars. In any case, if you're free tomorrow evening, around nine, come by the hotel at Furnace Creek. Casual, of course."

Claire was surprised but not displeased, and she was about to accept when she noticed a look on Raleigh's face. She hesitated, challenging his dour expression, and in that second, Sophie caught the nonverbal exchange.

"Oh, Raleigh... he's just being stiff," she confided. "He doesn't like me to include him as a host, although they're his friends too." She interrupted herself with a laugh, as if an inner joke couldn't wait. The humor

completely transformed her, smoothing the cool edges
and mellowing her otherwise over-polite speech. Claire
was still absorbing the change when Sophie composed
herself and went on.

"It's officially my party, but I'm sure Raleigh will be
glad to see you, too."

"Of course," he said, with a slight nod.

Claire wasn't so sure, but she did know that once
again he was treading a fine line of incivility, especially
after Sophie's warmth. She didn't see why Sophie would
want to invite her but it would be fun to go, if only to
antagonize Raleigh, so she smiled and accepted.

"You're welcome to bring a friend, of course," Sophie added.

It was a question of sorts, and perversely, Claire
would have liked to have the appropriate friend to bring
along. Knowing there was no one, she steadied her smile
and raised her chin slightly.

"Just me," she replied.

Sophie put out another languid hand as if that settled
all the business, and then headed for the Fiat.

"We'll see you later, then," she called over her narrow shoulder.

Raleigh looked thoughtful as he said his goodbyes,
and it was only as they drove off that Claire realized
what an impression she must have given. She was dressed
in her field gear, dusty from her morning on the cliffs of
Badwater, and with her hair trussed up in a favorite old
scarf. Her pockets bulged, and a pair of fishing glasses
hung on a granny necklace outside her collar. To put it
bluntly, she was a sight. Sophie had been perfectly and
tastefully dressed, cool despite the heat. The burned
mesquite had not been the only case of contrast. Suddenly she laughed, and an insight brought a twist to her

lips. She knew why she had been invited, and for that matter, she could guess why Sophie had become so friendly: it made her look charming when compared to the messy, monosyllabic geologist.

Claire paused to sit for a moment. The dust behind the car had already settled, and she almost wondered if she had imagined them. Sophie and Raleigh looked as if they had been dropped from another world, one of air conditioning and fine clothes and cocktail parties. It could have been hers, she knew, if she had given up her studies and played the game carefully. Never had the contrast of life-styles struck home so clearly.

But no. She had made the right choice. She could never have been content as a decoration on someone's elbow. She flipped open her notepad purposefully. It did no good to think of the past and could-have-beens; they only cluttered up the present.

She was productive the rest of the day, jotting notes and taking a few photographs of the riverbed. She was tempted to collect some samples, but it was illegal to remove even the tiniest pebble from a protected national monument. She'd stood firm about that when the committee suggested she selectively ignore the law, "just a little." Ultimately, the very point of the study was to protect and understand the strength and beauty that nature offered them. Was everyone crooked? She worked longer than she had intended, engrossed by the history enfolded in the terrain. It wasn't until nightfall that she got back to her trailer, and only then did she remember what was familiar about the rude man.

Raleigh Durban. The camera. He was a photographer, and a good one. Her friend who had helped with her darkroom had mentioned him, and she had seen some of his work reproduced in the Chicago Sunday

*Trib.* What would he be doing here? she wondered. The light camera he had carried today was hardly adequate for the quality of photography he would insist upon. On the other hand, it was unlikely he and Sophie had been merely touring around in such a remote spot. Even considering Sophie had a look that would qualify her as a model, Claire doubted they'd been doing a shoot. It didn't make sense. Her curiosity was nudged, and she smiled as she opened her traditional can of soup. She would enjoy discussing his work—that is, if they ever got to have a conversation that wasn't antagonistic or tediously polite. There was something challenging about his cool indifference and composure. He was so completely in control. She would like to see him surprised, or genuinely amused.

She shrugged. Both possibilities were equally unlikely. But it would be a nice gathering, a welcome change from her evening routine, and then she'd be back to her rocks.

Somehow that image was not as cheering as she expected.

## Chapter Two

The next morning was bright and clear, and Claire woke up to it with a half-asleep smile. She rolled over wondering why she felt so smug, and then sat bolt upright as she remembered what was coming up that evening. No matter what happened, she was going to a party. She hadn't dressed up for ages. Plummeting out of bed, she yanked open the closet and pulled out the suitcase that hunched on the floor inside.

At first sight, it was disappointing. The clothes she didn't need for her fieldwork were folded in neat, unencouraging piles. A pair of nice shoes looked distinctly drab. She hadn't packed intending to socialize, and the skirt and blouse were far more practical than she'd remembered. There was a pale-yellow scarf she had forgotten, but she could hardly appear in just a scarf that evening. The idea had a wicked appeal to it, though.

On impulse, Claire decided to spend the entire morning shopping; not that there was anywhere to shop, but

she could drive over to Shoshone and wander through
the little store. She needed to go there at some point
anyway to pick up some books she'd left with the ranger,
and the sixty-mile drive would be all the more bearable
if she knew there would be some fun at the end of it.
There was a rock shop there, too, with a tacky man who
offered her free rocks. It would be good to get out of the
valley for a day, and since she was ahead in her work, she
could afford the time. She smiled, knowing she was ra-
tionalizing, digging lamely for reasons to justify a friv-
olous day. Within a matter of minutes, she had showered
and was on the road. As she neared the date grove, Jolly
was setting up her stand, and Claire heard a grumble
from her neglected stomach. Jolly had seen her also, and
she'd be offended if Claire kept driving by without
stopping to say hello.

Jolly's Date Stand was one of the few genuinely quaint
places among the tourist mumbo-jumbo. This was due
largely to Jolly herself, whose good cheer and wander-
ing children were known up and down the valley. Claire
pulled over and stepped down just as Jolly succeeded in
setting up the folding table.

"Just a minute, honey," she called, and Claire waited
while she ran back through the date palms to her home
at the other end of the grove.

Jolly had a generous figure, and usually sat with her
light little feet barely touching the ground. When she
moved, which was rarely, she was surprisingly quick,
and Claire could easily imagine the lovely girl Juan
Avalos had fallen in love with many years before. Juan
ran the garage farther up the road, and one of their
children was always running back and forth between the
station and the date stand, carrying news and messages,
or just scattering dust for the fun of it.

Claire could see her coming back now, with a helpful son carrying a cloth sun umbrella behind her, and her own arms were full with Baggies, twist-ties and dates. Jolly had a good life, and a simple one. She let everyone know it, too, and when her example wasn't enough of a statement, she handed out advice in no uncertain terms. Claire had already been blessed with a sample of it, and had survived to come back and enjoy Jolly's comfortable friendship.

"You're still getting up early these days, huh?" she began. "When are you going to find someone to keep you up late so you sleep in? I tell you, Claire, you're too pretty to be getting up early in the morning." A big smile accompanied the words, and Claire had a hard time keeping her face straight as she reached for a Baggie. Together they bagged pounds and half-pounds of the sticky dates.

"You know how it is, Jolly. I've got my work to do. It's not everybody who has someone like Juan, and I wouldn't settle for less before giving up my work."

Jolly's eyes softened, and she instinctively looked up the road, as if to see her husband coming from the garage. Then she issued a low chuckle, which was her usual response to Claire's whimsy. It was an infectious noise, and Claire found herself grinning irrepressibly as Jolly launched into a sermon on men in general, and a man in particular, and how good work and late mornings should come in the proper proportions.

"All right, all right," Claire finally broke in. "Maybe you'll approve of me then. The only reason I'm up at all this morning is that I'm going shopping in Shoshone for a skirt or something. I, Claire Bennett, confirmed bachelorette, am going to a party tonight. Can you stand it? I've been invited to dessert up at the hotel. That should keep me up at least late enough so I'll sleep in a little tomorrow."

Jolly became serious.

"Up to the hotel? I've seen that crowd. I don't know, Claire."

Claire paused, holding a twist-tie in midair.

"What do you mean?" she asked.

"Well," Jolly said slowly, "there are some pretty flashy folks staying there right now. I'm not sure they're good enough for you."

"Don't you mean that the other way around?" Claire asked gently.

"Nope." She shook her grave head. "Some of those people have so much money they forget where it came from, and that's not good. They start thinking they're above everybody, and then they get careless and casual."

Jolly was more than usually serious this time, and Claire didn't know quite how to respond. She couldn't decide whether Jolly was expounding on a set of people she knew nothing about, or if she had in fact pinpointed the very thing that made Claire herself feel uncomfortable sometimes. For that matter, what did she know about Raleigh and Sophie? A light breeze brought the last of the early coolness to them, and Claire watched it ruffle the palm fronds while she considered.

Then Jolly was grinning again.

"What does an old woman know, you ask yourself," she said. "You go ahead and have a good time, honey. Tell Jason that Jolly sent you when you get to Shoshone, and pick out something you like. Not too wild, hear, just nice." She closed her eyes and brought her little hands together in a gesture of imagined perfection. Her eyes opened to smiling slits.

Claire smiled back, and dug up a dollar for a bag of dates.

"Yes, Jolly," she said obediently. "And I'll be very, very good," she added with a devious wink.

That startled Jolly chuckling again, and Claire left her twisting Baggies in the shade as she headed out of town. A brief glance told her no green Fiat was in the hotel parking lot, and then she was speeding south. She wondered what could have gotten Raleigh out so early, and doubted that the languid Miss Blake had been up to accompany him.

She put her mind on idle, rolled the windows all the way down, and caught an eleven-in-a-row country station on the radio. She passed signs for Echo Canyon, Pyramid Peak and Eagle Mountain. There were Indian names, too, for the Amargosa River and Shoshone itself. They intrigued the imagination. It was striking country, looking much the same as it must have when an ancient people had lived among its hills. If it weren't for the blacktop and her FM connection, she could easily have conjured up a lone scout heading off for the horizon. Shoshone came up sooner than she had expected. Only as she got out did she realize she had been getting stiff, and her eyes were tired from the glare.

Shoshone was a one-dog town. One dog, one Coke machine, one gas pump. The rock-shop man was sitting on his semicircular porch, just as she had seen him two months before. He greeted her as an old friend, but since he had greeted her that way the first time they had met also, she suspected he didn't really remember her. She was wrong, though, for he sauntered over to her car as she got out, and asked her how the geology was going.

"Pretty well," she replied. "I really only have another week's worth of stuff to do."

He leaned his face close to hers and whispered: "Better hurry. You wouldn't want anything to change before you could see it." A tobacco grin followed his joke, and he headed back to his shade. Funny old man. From his chair he could see every corner of the little town, and Claire doubted he missed anything.

It didn't take long to pick up her books from the ranger. He had put her boxload in the shed and forgotten all about it. They chatted a minute about the weather before he hurried off to answer a phone call.

It was not a job she envied. The rangers had a lot of territory they were responsible for, and their authority was ambiguous when tricky situations came up. The ranger from Furnace Creek, Mr. Ecks, had spent an evening telling her about the crime in the area. Many local jobs were filled by ex-convicts and others who might be just as pleased that the closest jail was two hundred miles away. He had promised to tell her about the suicides and missing persons the next time she came by. Claire knew he was only concerned for her safety, but she had managed to put off that next conversation. The Shoshone ranger's tired face had reminded her of it, and perhaps that was why she was suspicious when, upon returning to the front of the store, she noticed a rather scruffy-looking man hanging around the gas station. Usually she would never have even noted such a man, but now she watched him curiously, thinking he was uneasy and too intent upon looking up the empty road.

Shaking her head at her unprovoked mistrust, she entered a store with Jason's Sundries painted in block letters on a sign on the roof. The owner was out, but Jason Jr. smiled when she mentioned Jolly's name. He cradled his words with slow self-confidence.

"You want something a little special. I can see. Well, well. Why don't I just go look in the back for a minute? A skirt maybe, yes?"

Claire smiled. She had already realized it was unlikely she would find anything in the little store. It ran more to magazines and sunhats; cartoon T-shirts flaunting survival in Death Valley; spillproof coffee mugs and doughnuts in cellophane. She had found a rack in the corner with a couple of Mexican blouses on it when Jason Jr. reemerged.

"Maybe this is what you're looking for?"

Claire was amazed. Slung over one of his arms was a pile of lovely handmade skirts, woven in the soft hues of the desert at its best. Her eye was immediately drawn to one in a deep violet color, suggestive of the lingering light in the sky after the sun disappeared. She fingered the material, knowing that it would fall softly and feel cool. She would need to hand-wash it and iron it carefully for the rest of her days, but she already knew she would grow to love it. It was perfect for that evening.

"How did you know? Where did these come from?" she asked the young man. Her respect for Jason's Sundries had increased enormously.

He grinned slyly, managing to look very boyish.

"We have our secrets, you know. But for friends of Jolly, we like to have the best. You try this with some nice shoes and maybe a little frill on the blouse, and it will look very pretty, yes?"

Claire knew it would. By holding it against herself, she saw the adjustable waist made it unnecessary to try it on. She counted out her cash while he wrapped the skirt in a sheet of brown paper. Jason Jr. seemed to be just as delighted about the sale as she was about her find. She

was about to walk out when he stopped her, and she saw
with some surprise that he was blushing.

"You didn't happen to notice whether Jolly's daughter was home this morning, did you?"

So that was it. Claire ran over the date-stand encounter in her mind.

"I'm sorry, I don't know. I saw one of the sons, but it was still very early when I left Furnace Creek. Should I bring a message back for you or anything?"

He looked disappointed, but not dismayed.

"No, that's okay. I'll see her in a couple of days anyway, so you can just say hello to them all from Jason."

She would be glad to. With a goodbye, she walked out the door. So, she thought. Even here in the desert people manage to have something going on.

She was halfway across the street before she realized another car had pulled up next to her Scout. Quickly she looked around the street, for the familiar green Spider told her Raleigh must be nearby. It took her a minute to find him, standing unobtrusively in the shadow of the gas station. He was not alone. Even as she recognized the scruffy man she'd seen earlier, he stopped talking to Raleigh and hurried away behind the garage.

Claire started for her car, but Raleigh had seen her, and called as he walked over.

"We meet again."

"Very original."

They were both surprised by her tone.

"Almost as original as studying geology in a dime store."

"It's not a dime store," she said defensively. "And I'm taking the morning off, if it's any business of yours."

The man visibly withdrew, and Claire wondered at her own unfriendliness. Something about him irritated her, bringing out her worst, and now that she had been so abrupt, she couldn't ask why he was there too.

"I beg your pardon," he said, with unruffled graciousness.

Claire was suitably embarrassed, and felt the color creeping up her face. Now who was the boor?

"No, I'm sorry. I don't know why I said that. I just came to do a little shopping. It was a hot drive," she ended lamely. She sounded like a schoolgirl to her own ears. He must think she was an idiot.

He watched her as if to figure out her words, and then he smiled.

"Don't worry," he said. "It's perfectly natural to be caught shopping in Shoshone—fashion capital that it is. It can happen to the best of us."

She laughed, and her mirth erased the tension between them.

"You'll have to promise not to tell, now that you've discovered my big secret."

He smiled. They were standing in the middle of the street, where the glare off the dirt road made it especially hot. There was no reason to linger, and she turned to move toward the cars. He spoke quickly.

"How would you like—? I don't know. Can I buy you a drink or something? I never thanked you properly for offering to help me out the other night."

She was surprised, and unaccountably pleased.

"I am rather thirsty," she admitted.

He nodded and they looked expectantly at the town around them. There was no bar or restaurant to be seen. An image of a glass-fronted refrigerator in Jason's surfaced in Claire's mind, but she instantly dismissed it.

He'd made the invitation. Let him come up with the lo-
cation. He was grinning.

"Let me make that a Coke," he said. "Right this
way."

With elaborate courtesy, he led her over to the Coke
machine outside the gas station. It hummed loudly in the
heat, and the cans came out cold and slippery. A lone
picnic table sat under a tamarack tree to the left of the
station, and they were soon seated, leaning their backs
against the table and stretching their legs out before
them. They faced the town, which shimmered in the
heat. The rock man was a gray lump in the shade of his
porch, and from somewhere a radio sang thinly.

"God, that's good," Raleigh said, resting his can on
his knee. He wiped his temple with the back of his hand
and Claire felt the perspiration at the back of her own
neck. It was hot, no question about that, but neither the
heat nor the drink could account for the light churning
in her stomach. Here they were, sitting together like old
friends. It felt like the most natural thing in the world,
but this old friend was a complete stranger.

She stole glances at the man next to her, starting with
the neat black shoes that stretched out farther than her
own dusty ones. His legs were clad in comfortable khaki,
and when they shifted and resettled, they hinted of the
muscular power hidden there in repose. His shirt was a
soft gray, and the narrow shoulder strap of his camera
slung a tight black line across his chest. She glanced
briefly at his face, hoping her scrutiny had gone unnoticed, and resisting the desire to study him even more
carefully.

He was looking up the street, shaking his head.

"I'd go completely insane in a place like this," he
stated.

"It is a little slow-paced," Claire allowed.

"'Slow-paced!' 'Comatose' is more like it. When the rock man blinks, it's news."

She chuckled.

"I take it you're not from the country."

"Manhattan," he answered simply, taking another long swallow from his can. What on earth could have brought him here, she wondered. Sophie must be one strong attraction.

"It's not that bad," she said. "Not counting Shoshone, I mean; I wouldn't do anything but shop in Shoshone. But the desert itself is really something."

"I don't know a thing about it," he said. "It all looks foreign to me. Like something from a movie. Not real. It fascinates me, but only as something to watch from a distance, from a safe distance. Did you say you were a naturalist?"

"I'm a geologist," she said, somewhat disappointed. She'd been unusually interested in everything about him, and he couldn't even recall her profession. It wasn't exactly flattering. It was more worthy of a laugh, actually, and she smiled.

"What's so funny?" he asked.

"Nothing," she said. Then she improvised on another tack. "Maybe Shoshone is the whole world to the rock man there. I'll bet he knows every bump in the road, and notices every visitor who comes, just like you know the best taxi corners in the city. People fill up their lives with different details—whatever's convenient, and whatever it takes until they have enough...Shoshone or Manhattan." She shrugged. "You might say it's arbitrary. Know what I mean?"

"I'd almost buy that," he said, "except that I'd damn well rather have Manhattan." He grinned warmly. "Shoshone's a great place to visit, but . . ."

She found herself laughing back, and admitted to herself he had his own brand of humor. She swallowed the last of her drink, closing her eyes as it coursed down her throat. He watched her, and when her eyes opened, she was caught in the intensity of his gaze. Her eyes met his frankly, and a thrill jarred through her. There was a complete subtext of another conversation going on beneath the things they were saying, as if the easy exchanges on top were camouflage for a deeper connection. He shifted and stood up.

"You look like you could drink another one of those." His voice was lower, and she wondered if he had been thinking the same thing.

"No, that's all right," she answered. "I should be getting back anyway." She lifted her parcel and some of the violet material of the skirt slid out from the loose wrapping. She quickly caught it up, but not before Raleigh had seen it.

"You really weren't kidding," he remarked.

Claire blushed and eyed the incriminating parcel.

"No. I don't have anything else, and I didn't think my overalls would do for 'Dessert in the Desert,' even if it is casual."

They walked toward the cars, and Raleigh smiled, trying to remember something.

"Is that what you had on yesterday?"

"No," she laughed. "That was some other equally unsuitable outfit. I save the overalls for special occasions."

He seemed to consider.

"Well, I thought you looked nice," he said with disarming honesty.

It was so unexpected, Claire laughed aloud. He looked questioningly at her.

"You're very kind to say so, I'm sure," she said, "but I can't say I admire your taste. Now, if you'll say I look nice tonight, or maybe 'ravishing,' *that* I might appreciate."

He gave a wry twist to his lips.

"What if I don't?"

Unexpected again. Claire caught her breath. They reached their cars and stepped into the narrow space between them, suddenly close. Claire had to look up to see his face. He was waiting for a reply.

"I'll be crushed," she asserted, and wondered if it might even be true.

"Perhaps a small bribe of some kind would be in order," he suggested, containing a smile.

That was more like him. She put mock shock on her face and turned to her car. She fit the key in the lock and opened the door, sliding her package across the seat. She felt him watching her, and looked over her shoulder to give a mischievous smile.

"Knowing you, it would more likely be blackmail. I wonder if you threaten everybody, on principle." She didn't realize how her low voice added provocative weight to the words.

She pivoted to step into her car, but even more quickly, he reached an arm around her waist and pulled her against him. Before she knew it, he had turned her with a dexterity she could not resist, and pinned her in a tight embrace.

"Only when they throw me a challenge," he said, with a quizzical smile. The flicker in his eyes went beyond teasing.

Startled, Claire looked up into his face, and felt an excitement that wasn't due simply to the suddenness of the gesture. She was breathless, and keenly aware of the length of his body against hers. An eternity passed. She saw the expression in his eyes change, making them an almost piercing blue, and then he bent his head and kissed her.

As if by instinct, she felt herself responding, irresistibly drawn to him. A tremor rocked her body, and then realization hit her like panic. Quickly, she turned her face and tried to push away from him. The circle of his arms tightened, restraining her, and she looked up briefly to see a question in his eyes. Her emotional confusion was topped off by a sting behind her eyelids, and she pushed him again with renewed urgency.

"Let me go," she whispered, and he did, gently.

She braced herself against the car, distracted and flushed, and anxiously scanned the street. Jason Jr. had stepped out on the store porch and was deliberately looking off toward the distant hills. The rock man was staring at them with undisguised interest. Raleigh saw the direction of her gaze, and smiled at her.

"We wouldn't want to cause a scene now, would we?" he said, in a conspiratorially low voice.

Her heart was still thudding dangerously, and her mind circled, trying to absorb what had happened. Her nerves registered his amusement, and it bolstered her enough so she could straighten her shoulders and put on a semblance of composure. She would have preferred to melt into the street. Jason Jr. was now shifting awkwardly, watching them, and she could see he held something in his hand.

"What is it, Jason?" she called.

He looked relieved and walked over, holding out her sunglasses.

"You forgot these," he offered.

She stepped to take them from him, and he strode back to the store.

Raleigh was leaning against his car and the tension between them had broken, leaving the air especially hot and soundless. His smile was casual, yet she thought she caught a glimpse of concern beneath it. Silently, he leaned forward to reopen her door for her, and held it as she stepped past him and got in. He waited for her to roll down her window. Their positions echoed their first meeting at the side of the road, and Claire felt a blush stealing up her cheeks yet another time. The blush irritated her, and Raleigh laughed.

"That's better. I was worried there for a minute, but now I can see you're annoyed at something again. Let's see," he paused, with exaggerated self-consciousness. "Perhaps my tie's not straight."

He wasn't even wearing a tie. Claire was not amused.

"It couldn't have anything to do with the fact that a strange man just forced a kiss on me," she said.

His smile stiffened.

"Oh, come on. I know what I see. We both knew it was coming."

"But why didn't you let me go when—" she stopped, remembering her panic. She couldn't understand it herself.

"Of course. And make a really noteworthy scene. Two lovers kissing is one thing. Two lovers fighting publicly is quite another."

Claire was stung.

"That's just great. I suppose that's why you're still talking to me now," she said, jerking a thumb in the direction of the rock shop. "Putting up a charade of a sweet goodbye. Next you'll expect me to thank you, sweetheart." The last word was an expressive hiss.

Raleigh spun quickly on his heel, and slammed the door as he got into his car. Before Claire could maneuver the big Scout out of her parking space, Raleigh's Fiat was sending the hot dust flying. She shifted gears roughly, and ignored the rock man's impudent wave as she took off.

Had he apologized? Oh no. Not him. He'd kissed her as if it were his right. He'd barged right in and taken her up on her challenge when she hadn't even known she'd issued one. Then he'd flung the responsibility for it in her face.

Her light spirits of the morning were replaced by fury, and Claire blushed to herself as she remembered his kiss. Of all the nerve! She had been moved, no doubt about it, and she hadn't denied that she'd wanted him to kiss her. The man had a smoothness all his own, and she found him more attractive than she wanted to admit. He provoked something more, too: a kind of energy or stimulation that she felt when they were together. It pervaded even their simplest exchanges, keeping her on an edge of expectation. Even so, it had started to come forward with a passion she could not have anticipated, and in that second of response, she had been frightened by the intensity of her own feelings. What had started as a flirtatious exchange had jolted something she had forgotten even existed. If it ever had. It was bewildering, but rather wonderful. A slim smile tugged at the corners of her mouth. Was she offended or intrigued? She had been alone too long. The habit of arguing both sides of everything with herself had added an annoying flexibility to her otherwise decisive mind.

What did she know about Raleigh? He was a rude, arrogant man. She didn't even know what he had been doing in Shoshone and somehow this irritated her. She thought back. He had had his camera with him again, but she hadn't seen him take any photos. He was an odd sort of tourist to be covering the kind of ground he obviously did. What had he been saying to that peculiar man? Perhaps he had gone there to meet him. Perhaps he didn't want his reasons known and he had intentionally gotten her involved to distract attention.

Claire was amazed at herself. She was not a suspicious person, and yet here she was being a detective about some flashy guy who had given her a kiss. Again something stirred inside her, and she knew she was going to be curious as long as she had the chance to find out more about him.

Sophie's party. Raleigh would be acting as an unofficial host. If he was as intimate with the hostess as had been implied, he shouldn't have been free to kiss her, no matter how spontaneously.

Her heart sobered to a moderate pace as she remembered Jolly's comment. Maybe Raleigh was just careless. Maybe he was amusing himself by teasing a tactless, harmless geologist who had stumbled conveniently across his path. A corner of her mind protested, but she straightened her arms against the wheel and leveled her eyes on the road. She wasn't going to be anybody's little lark, not even if "anybody" could kiss her as he had.

# *Chapter Three*

Claire slipped on a soft cream-colored blouse and smoothed the violet skirt over her hips. The coolness of the evening and a long shower had combined to make her feel more than usually physically alive. Now she looked forward to the party at the hotel with a slight nervousness. She hadn't gotten dressed up for anything for ages, it seemed, and she abandoned herself to enjoying her preparation as much as possible. She knew from past experiences that getting ready for a festivity was often more fun than the event itself.

Even without a full-length mirror, Claire was sure the new material fell gracefully, and she took a swish around the trailer, relishing the forgotten movement of a full skirt. She picked up the yellow scarf and tied it around her waist. Hands on hips, she paused, and then slowly untied it again. She had expected the complementary colors to work together, but now she saw their closeness was too abrupt. Instead she draped the scarf loosely around her neck, liking the silkiness, and with a glance in the mirror, decided it would have to do. After a brush of mascara on her lashes, she was ready. Her instinct for simplicity served her well, for the soft yellow against her throat echoed the gold highlights in her auburn hair while intensifying the depths of her eyes. She chuckled to herself. No one could accuse her of trying to outshine the hostess, but in her own subtle way, she was striking, and she had the confidence to know it.

Anxiousness joined her again as she pulled into the hotel parking lot. It was just after nine, but she could hear a number of voices on the terrace already as she mounted the low steps to the lobby. The clerk had just directed her toward the voices when Sophie, clad in a shimmer of aqua, leaned in the French doors and called to her.

"There you are. So glad you could make it. Come in and meet some of this crazy bunch."

Claire put her courage into her smile and stepped onto the terrace. A number of couples were scattered over the tiled floor, sipping cocktails and talking in sophisticated murmurs. They looked anything but crazy. A single glance sufficed to tell her Raleigh wasn't present, and at the periphery of her mind she was both disappointed and relieved. There were not quite a dozen people in all, and from some intangible feeling of intimacy in the way they gestured and handed each other drinks, Claire immediately grasped that they knew each other from somewhere else. They'd been picked up and plopped in the desert, complete with friends of friends and small world acquaintances. With one exception: Claire felt a gentle surge of relief as she recognized the familiar face of the ranger, Mr. Ecks, who was talking animatedly to an elegantly dressed woman at the edge of the party.

After meeting Sophie's immediate circle of guests and accepting a small glass of something cold, she moved over to Mr. Ecks. He wore his beige ranger's uniform and seemed determined to maintain the "casual" part of the invitation. He had a wicked way of laughing at people without their knowing it, and he particularly relished doing it when the person in question thought she was laughing at him. It was certainly an original way to amuse himself, and the woman he'd picked was a perfect victim. Once Claire was in on his game, she watched, sometimes shocked at his audacity, while he numbly regaled Ms. Boothman with the perils of the desert. Claire relaxed with the humor.

She leaned against the railing, physically removing herself halfway from the conversation, and took a moment to look more carefully around the terrace. It really was lovely. Several tables had been set out with coffee and drinks, and one had an inviting silver bowl filled with fruit. Little dishes of chocolates and mints took turns with a row of cake slices. Low garden candles and votives were set in groups among the dishes and around the plants, and their light catching on a leaf or bit of silver visually dared the cool of the night to invade the terrace. The effect was subdued, but very classy, and Claire easily assumed it had been Sophie's idea. She would have liked to memorize it, or take a picture.

Raleigh was still not among the guests. She looked again, but his height would have betrayed him in an instant, so he was certainly not there. It was odd, considering he was a friend of Sophie's and was acting as a host of sorts. She was going to mention it to Mr. Ecks and was waiting for a discreet pause in his farfetched conversation, when an undistinguished young man approached and leaned on the railing next to her.

"You're Miss Bennett, aren't you? Sophie introduced us back there, but I didn't get a chance to say a
proper hello. I'm Jake Bowing."

A shy, companionable smile followed the soft-spoken
introduction, and Claire found herself warming to him.
His suit was nondescript, but he wore a hideous tie that
could have been the gift of an insipid godmother. Claire
had hardly noticed him among the group near Sophie,
but now she saw the blond, fine-featured man had a
distinctive gentleness behind his glasses.

"Of course," she said. "You're the astronomer,
right? It looks like we're going to have an excellent night
to see some of the stars. It's best when there isn't a
moon, isn't it?"

Jake nodded, and with a little coaxing, began to tell
her of his work at the planetarium and conservatory.
Claire soon realized that he spent most of his time
studying and doing research and, though obviously intelligent, he was not used to chatting at this type of social engagement. She smiled to herself. Perhaps she
looked as self-conscious herself, and she thought, wryly,
that Sophie might have sent Jake over so they could take
care of each other. True or not, the thought spurred her
determination to enjoy herself, and she devoted herself
to drawing out the shy astronomer. She soon discovered
in him an unexpected and subtle sense of humor that
thrived on understatement. With this key, it was only a
matter of minutes until they were laughing quietly like
old friends, and Claire only noticed just how quickly the
time was going when Sophie stepped forward and
clapped her hands.

"All right, everyone. The night has been very oblig-
ing, you'll notice, and the stars have come out. It might
help if you take off your shades now, George."

Her audience chuckled politely as George removed the offending sunglasses. People settled into the chairs and leaned against the adobe supports as she drew Jake into the middle of the terrace.

"Most of you have met Jake Bowing, I think," she began, and soon Jake had the floor. His mellow voice was distinct but not overloud, and his audience had to listen carefully as he led them across the sky.

Claire stepped into a deeper shadow where she could see Jake's profile and the other guests, while getting the clearest view of the sky. She leaned her hip against a low wall and crossed her arms in reply to the light breeze.

Never had she seen the heavens so bright with lights. Draco and Andromeda became lost in the myriad of stars as she gazed, spellbound, mesmerized by the gentle drone of Jake's voice. His words, the terrace and even the time slipped away from her, leaving her solitary, until only the stars and the wind seemed real. Unnervingly real. Was everything like this in the desert? Magical, and a little bit frightening? Why did she constantly have the feeling that something was about to happen?

Someone was laughing, and Claire heard Jake say: "But of course, private lessons are available."

Claire tuned in to see him smiling gallantly at one of the guests, apparently responding to her question.

"I'm at your service," he volunteered.

The other guests laughed, and Jake caught Claire's eye to wink before he turned back to answer another question.

"At your service too, no doubt," said a low voice behind Claire.

Startled, she turned, and found Raleigh had moved behind her and was standing close. He seemed taller than ever in the shadow, and his tieless collar was open at the neck. She tried to collect her poise as she considered his words. He must have caught Jake's wink but missed the humor.

"How long have you been there?" she asked him, annoyed at the surprise still evident in her voice.

"Oh, I snuck in some time around Draco's tail star. That's quite the skyful we have there, isn't it? It would take several private lessons to get it all straight, don't you think?" There was something coy in his tone, and she wished she could see his face so she could be sure he was insinuating what she suspected.

"Perhaps," she said. "Perhaps not." What did he expect her to say? *Jake and I already have ten lessons signed up. Care to join us?* Hardly.

All the ease she had achieved deserted her. She couldn't begin to banter with this man. It had been so much easier to talk with Jake, where the tension had not shot back and forth between them. Now, even as she and Raleigh stood together silently, it was an uncomfortable silence, made even more so by the intimacy of the dim lighting. He must have felt it too, for he shifted, and drew a little farther from her. She could think of absolutely nothing to say, and as a host, semi- or otherwise, he wasn't doing much of a job himself.

From across the terrace, she heard Sophie's laughter, and a moment later the outdoor spots came on, strategically pushing back the darkness without highlighting any particular part of the terrace. Claire breathed more easily, but now she could see Raleigh was frowning at her.

"Now what have I done to annoy you?" she asked, taking a step toward a railing the light had revealed. Instead of leaning against it with her, he pivoted in front of her, putting his back to the rest of the guests.

"I was wondering the same thing. I pick astronomy, the most conspicuous and innocuous topic available, and you have nothing to say about it."

Claire shot a look at his eyes, but they were laughing now, and clearly invited her to share in their amusement. Had she misread his implications, or had he turned the tables once again? She was about to dismiss the earlier undercurrent, when his eyelids lowered slightly.

"Or could it be you thought I meant something else?" He went on. "We seem to have a gift for misunderstanding each other, don't we?"

"Especially when you're insinuating things," she said, before she could stop herself. Instantly he stiffened. He didn't disagree, but her tone had drastically altered the flavor of the exchange. He grew overly polite and removed.

"But then you clear things up for us, don't you?"

He shifted sideways, opening his view to include the terrace again, and absently scanned the crowd.

Claire was mortified. She was never rude like that, and now, as a guest, at a party she'd been enjoying more than she ever expected to, she had tactlessly peppered her host in a most childish way. Quite unprovoked for once, too. She would have liked to sit him down and really clear things up for once. Instead she was always guessing, unable to reply to his sophisticated innuendos. She felt a blush staining her cheeks, and yet, she could not bring herself to apologize. It was that stubborn, proud streak surfacing again. She'd have to do something about it. The situation became more ridiculous with each passing second, and she groped desperately for anything to say that might dispel the discomfort that weighed in the air between them.

"Do you intend to visit Shoshone again soon?"

The words were barely past her teeth when the image they summoned brought a deeper blush beneath her tan. No subject was safe, it seemed. Fortunately Raleigh had a sense of humor, and his cool exterior melted somewhat.

"Why? Do you intend to meet me there?" he countered.

"Sure, and we can call out the whole town next time to make sure they witness our rendezvous."

She smiled and he laughed softly.

"It should take weeks just to write up the invitations," he said.

Their eyes caught, and in the instant, the dynamics between them changed again. She looked away, aware of a gentle burning in her cheeks, while her mind tried to follow what had happened. Without being conspicuous, Raleigh slipped his hand onto the railing behind her. It suggested an embrace without really being one, and Claire decided to pretend she didn't notice it. He was smiling at her now, and she felt something tug at her insides.

"I believe the word is 'ravishing,'" he said.

The compliment was betrayed by a wicked gleam in his eye, and it would have been impossible to misconstrue his teasing. Claire acknowledged the thrust and instinctively parried.

"But how unkind of you!" she replied, in dulcet tones.

"I beg your pardon?"

"When you know what lengths I went to to find something for this event, and then all you can come up with is 'ravishing'—like a bribed parrot or something."

He chuckled appreciatively.

"Modesty," he said. "Modesty, please."

An eruption of laughter came across the terrace from where Sophie was entertaining. Her color was heightened and her face was animated, but for the first time that evening, Claire sensed that her hostess was not enjoying herself. She wondered why.

"Do you often have parties like this?" she asked Raleigh.

He followed her gaze toward Sophie and paused. She regretted the question, for it caused him to withdraw slightly.

"Sophie does. I am often invited but I usually can't come. It must seem strange, I suppose, but imagine having already done everything; every kind of amusement. You've already been to the Virgin Islands, Aspen, Newport Beach . . . I don't know. You start looking for something unusual to do, and when someone suggests a cozy get-together in Death Valley, you figure, 'Well, why not?'" He frowned for a second. "They're a harmless crowd. Maybe a little boring and selfish, but not any more so than anyone else."

He gave an impartial shrug, and let his eyes stray over his friends. Claire found his detachment unsettling. Was he so jaded, so indifferent to his friends? Was he unaware of the picture he had painted? Their lives sounded wasteful to her, but sad, too. She stared at Sophie's laughing crowd, unsure whether to pity or despise them. Her mouth twisted at the paradox of having too much. He sensed her disapproval.

"You're thinking it's unfair? Maybe. I think of it more as their luck, or their misfortune."

"Then, you don't include yourself with them?" she asked.

He eyed her, and she wondered if she had offended him. Then he gave a brief smile.

"No," he said simply. "Would you?"

"Never," she declared, a little too vehemently.

Raleigh watched her curiously. She hoped she wouldn't have to explain. Her response was instinctive, a combination of her own disapproval and a reaction to his indifference. Imagine having done everything! Why, there'd be no point!

"I can see you wouldn't, come to think of it," he said lightly. "Wardrobe problems aside, I don't think decadent living would be quite your style."

She smiled. He did understand, and her frank eyes thanked him with silent eloquence. She inadvertently leaned back, and the solid pressure of his arm seared through the light material of her blouse. A startled gasp escaped her as she leaned forward again, and then she blushed vividly for her reaction. It was only his arm against her back, for heaven's sake! No need to be as jumpy as a cat hit by lightning. Raleigh was keenly aware of what had happened, and from the corner of her eye, Claire tried to gauge his reaction. He leaned closer and settled his arm neatly around her waist, smiling defiantly down at her.

"You shouldn't be allowed to wear pretty clothes," he said. His lowered voice resonated, and his eyes shone dark with approval. Claire's head took a spin. The warmth from his arm was stealing through the rest of her body, making it difficult to breathe properly, and she had the disconcerting impression he was enjoying his impact. Annoyance rapidly caught up with Claire's surprise and commotion.

He smiled wryly and slid his arm away. Sophie was slipping through the shadows toward them, and Claire quickly took a step back.

"Captivating another guest, Ral?" Sophie said easily.

The aqua gown clung suggestively to her figure, and she slid her hand into Raleigh's in the possessive little gesture Claire had seen before. The smile she extended to Claire lacked the warmth that it had held when she'd first arrived.

"I don't mean to intrude," she said, "but I believe some of the guests are ready to go, and we should say goodbyes." Her sleepy-lidded eyes missed nothing.

"Of course," he said, and looked over his shoulder. During the instant his head was turned, Claire caught the full brunt of Sophie's green eyes.

"I—I really must be going myself," Claire said. "I have to get up early, but this has been a delightful evening. Thank you for thinking to invite me, Sophie."

Sophie flashed another smile and Claire got a better chance to see how hollow it was.

"It's not every day the local geologist turns out to make such a charming guest." Her compliment was issued more as a challenge, and Claire would not have been surprised to see her clutch more closely to Raleigh's arm. The jealousy, however misplaced, was thinly veiled.

Jake and a couple of the other guests had come up, and overheard the last exchange without perceiving the undercurrent. Jake smiled at Sophie and then at Claire. His eyes were candid and warm.

"That's for sure," he said. "Where do you plan to study tomorrow, Claire?"

She found herself the center of attention, and was relieved to be on safer ground. She could think over Sophie's behavior later.

"I'm doing a check on Ubehebe Crater. It's up north, and the check is really rather routine, since that area has been researched beyond belief. It's an interesting place, though, and I've looked forward to seeing it."

"You know how it is with those craters," Jake said, suddenly serious. "You've seen one, you've seen them all."

Claire laughed with the others, and was thankful once again that Jake's good humor put everyone at ease. That was a real gift. They shook hands and said goodbyes all around, and Claire scanned the remaining guests, hoping to catch Mr. Ecks before he left. She thought she saw his back when Raleigh took a pause from his hostly duties to lean toward her.

"Do you mind having company while you work?" he asked.

Claire didn't understand, and her surprise obviously told him so.

"I've been meaning to visit Ubehebe myself, and I could join you if I wouldn't be disturbing your work."

"Not at all," she said. "I'll be there around four."

He nodded and didn't say any more, and in a moment, Claire had been swept out with the last group of guests. Mr. Ecks must have been watching for her, too, for she met him at the bottom of the steps outside the hotel.

"Did you have a nice time, Claire?"

"To my surprise, I did," she answered.

Mr. Ecks looked pleased with himself.

"I did too. They're good people if you don't get too close," he said, with one of his mocking smiles. The intensity of his gaze belied his humor, however, and Claire sensed he was trying to warn her, or to ask her something in his roundabout way.

"You don't need to worry about me," she reassured him, wondering if she looked so much as if she needed someone to watch over her. That seemed to be what he wanted to hear, however, for he said goodbye and left her standing in the now very dark night.

## Chapter Four

The sand dunes spread like hills of snow, interrupted only by the daring mesquite, growing twisted in occasional clumps. The hot, endless sand would be the delight of any barefoot child, and Claire had left her shoes back in the car, succumbing to the abandon that accompanies the liberated foot. Without a wind, the dunes were still and bright. Not even the shadow of an insect challenged the glitter, and Claire slipped on her sunglasses to cover her squint.

She had packed a sandwich and an orange earlier that morning. Now she sat down, and pulled these out of her satchel. She had just stopped at Stovepipe Wells for a bottle of cold cider and, indulging an impulse, she had bought an ice-cream sandwich. Since this was well on the way to becoming a wet mess, she started her lunch with dessert, licking her fingers and smiling to herself. *If Sophie could see me now,* she thought, remembering her hostess's cool veneer from the night before. *I've re-*

*verted to being the five-year-old on the beach.* That was what she felt like—a giant baby—and the generic dunes offered no scale to tell her otherwise.

Her turkey and Swiss tasted like a feast, seasoned with a good appetite and the great outdoors. As she finished peeling her orange, she pulled out a slim pile of letters she'd picked up from general delivery at the post office. She wished she had noticed the return addresses sooner, as she ripped open the envelope from Earthquakes, Inc.

The letter was short, and handwritten, and she glanced quickly at the signature. Harris. The name stirred some feeling inside her, something she didn't take the time to examine, but that wasn't warm. He would be coming, he said, around the sixteenth, to see if she needed any final help and to pick up some of the equipment and reference books they had lent her. He would call the hotel and leave a message when he knew more clearly when he would be driving in, or, if she wouldn't be at hand, he would check her trailer in the evening when she would be back. There was nothing personal, but his tone assumed an intimacy, a casualness that irked her. Claire shoved the letter back into her satchel and made a face. She had expected the committee to check up on her, and at times she would have appreciated another opinion and an extra pair of eyes, but she had carried through doggedly on her own, and it was offensive to have someone swing through now, almost haphazardly even, rather than professionally. She shrugged. That was how things went. She could drive off on the fourteenth, or irresponsibly misplace, say, the enlarger. A corner of her thought the mischief would be just what they needed, but she knew she would do nothing intentionally to offend Harris or his committee; their good recommendation was too vital to her career.

The other letter was a note from Uncle Chaz, hoping she was fine and managing to express his doubt of it at the same time. That was him all over. He might never understand geology was more intriguing to her than the furniture business, but he was a dear. There was also a Manhattan postcard from an old roommate wondering what had become of her. It had been forwarded, and Claire decided to send a proper reply the next time she got a chance to sit down and write. She still couldn't imagine her wild, decadent sidekick in business attire.

Checking her watch, she stood up and collected the wrapper and peels from around her. In a few hours, the dunes would be suffused in shadows, abstracted even more by the oranges of the sunset. It would have been nice to laze around. She put on her shoes and soon the trusty Scout was rumbling beneath her.

Claire felt good. She would reach Ubehebe just before four, and she could spend the remainder of the afternoon prowling around and maybe hiking to Little Ubehebe nearby. She started to whistle—a tune that had nothing to do with what the radio was playing—and then she laughed. Admit it, you goose, she thought. You're looking forward to seeing Raleigh. It was true. She didn't bother looking at it any closer than that. It was enough to be driving along, feeling pleased with the whole world. Well, not quite the whole world. Deliberately, she put Harris's letter out of her mind, and dedicated the remaining drive to humming and noticing how pretty the hills had become.

She arrived at Ubehebe and Raleigh's Fiat was nowhere to be seen. Stepping out of the car into a light wind, she strode to the brim of the crater and looked down the slopes of the six-hundred-foot bowl. Ubehebe meant "Big Basket" in Shoshone, and that was indeed

what it looked like. Technically, it wasn't a crater at all,
but a maar left over from an explosion within the earth
years before. The sight beckoned her to run straight
down, as if it were instinct to go exploring, and she could
barely contain her impatience as she waited for Raleigh.
When her minute hand crept past the hour, her annoyance grew with each tap of her foot, and she tried to ignore her sense of disappointment. If he wasn't going to
come, he shouldn't have volunteered in the first place.
She scuffed the gravel and walked back to the Scout.
After one last look down the road, she slung her gear
over her shoulder and started down the steep trail. As
soon as she was below the brim, the wind stopped and a
stillness weighed heavily around her. Again she paused,
listening, and then grimly she smiled to herself. She had
never been stood up on a crater date before.

Along the walls of the crater, the ranger service had
posted signs warning the adventurous not to try to climb
the maar walls. Mr. Ecks had told her that an occasional tourist would start scaling the rocky slopes and
then be unable to make his way back down. The shale
and gravel were prone to unexpected slides and it took an
expert team of rock climbers, rangers and sometimes
even a helicopter to rescue the stranded person. She
could see why. The slopes of the bowl looked deceptively easy to scale, and the invitation to photographers
and the merely curious was tempting. It was a case of the
mountain being there.

She kept checking back over her shoulder, but the
short horizon from within the crater remained clear of
Raleigh's tall frame. It took her several minutes to reach
the base, which was level and cracked with dried mud.
The backs of her legs ached from the constant down-
ward walking, and she was glad to sit down on a big

rock. The heat penetrated her thin blouse and she instinctively reached for her sunscreen. The silence picked up her tiniest noises, and coconut filtered aromatically into the air around her. Now that the exercise had routed the disappointment from her system, she felt quite at home. *I must have a thing for solitude,* she thought. *I'll have to try one of those sensory deprivation tanks sometime.*

Flipping open her notebook, she began making notes. The work absorbed her for quite some time, and when she finally surfaced long enough to check her watch, she was startled to see it was nearly a quarter to five. It seemed earlier, but her skin felt the time in the sun. She'd forgotten all about Raleigh, but now she wondered whether he had really stood her up or if he had had trouble on the road. He didn't have much luck with his flashy car. She checked the trail again, but it remained relentlessly empty.

The whole bowl was completely empty, for that matter, and suddenly the stillness took on an unworldly quality. She felt an urge to get out, and nearly jumped when a shadow passed over the crater. High above, a jet was speeding south. She knew an air-force base bordered Death Valley on the south side, but she also knew that jets were not permitted to fly over the Monument. Some hotshot air cadet, no doubt. Claire stepped back a couple of paces and shaded her eyes to follow the line of flight. It was soon out of sight, cutting so high she hadn't heard even a distant roar. Things were strange here.

"Hey!" she yelled, but the sound was immediately absorbed.

"Am I alone?" she asked the walls. The words fell flat to her feet, numb. She walked across the floor of the basin, kicking stones and finally throwing one. It hit the wall, trickled a bit and then lay still. She took a step nearer, surveying the slope closely. It seemed to twist before her eyes, a trick angle in an otherwise unrelieved shell. She slung her Canon AE1 securely over her shoulder and started up the most solid part of the crater wall, keeping an eye on the unusual crevice. She had been warned too many times, and she would be careful not to climb too high. Still, when she paused to look back, she was surprised to see she was already farther up than she had thought. She stopped, and settled herself on a rain-cut ledge for a couple of photos. She lifted the camera higher, focusing on the opposite rim. Through the lens, a moving spike appeared on the flawless edge and was magnified into the sudden shape of a man. With a twinge of nervousness and guilt, she took a quick shot with her camera and lowered it.

On the far side, the man had spied her and was quickly descending the trail. Claire started carefully down the slope, moving slowly and taking no risks with her footing. *Wouldn't you know it,* she thought. *I've been alone and getting the creeps for an hour, and the second I do something questionable, somebody else materializes just in time to see it.* In the silence of the basin, she could hear the man's footsteps on the gravel, and between the crunching noises, she could hear his voice, without making out the words. She inwardly groaned as she recognized the tone. She had almost reached the level ground and safety when Raleigh stepped off the bottom of the trail and began to cross over to her. From his expression, she could see that he was not pleased, and her guilt and the danger of what she had done caused her to feel defensive before he opened his mouth.

"What do you think you're doing? Only an idiot would climb up there. Can't you read?"

He was actually pointing to the sign.

"Of course I can read," she yelled back, her voice unusually high. "I know what I'm doing. I didn't go very far up and I was very careful."

As if to prove her point, she took a bold step forward. It was the one uncalculated movement of her entire descent, and the poor footing suddenly slid out from under her. She gave a startled cry and put out her hands to stop her fall. Raleigh sprang forward, but not before she landed full force on her left hand and shoulder. The camera jarred against a rock. Wincing, and afraid to move in case it would hurt, she lifted her head and looked into his face. He was very pale as he knelt next to her, his eyes searching. When he saw she could see him and looked coherent, he held on to her free shoulder and gently helped her to sit up.

"Don't move," he ordered.

Claire had no desire to move, and as he touched her arm experimentally, she cringed and pulled back.

"All right, I know I was stupid, but you don't have to jerk me around."

Despite herself, the tears welled up in her eyes as the initial shock wore off and she felt real pain running in shoots down to her wrist. Her palm stung where it had skidded in the dust, and she sat staring at it. Raleigh had ignored her comment, and now he slid his arm deliberately behind her good shoulder and lifted her to her feet. The maneuver was anything but smooth.

"Come on. You're probably fine, but we have to get back as quickly as possible anyway. Do you have any other gear?" he asked, eyeing the camera.

"Just my sack. It's over there," she said, nodding to her things, and trying to retuck her shirt with her good hand. She stood unsteadily as he slid her sack over his elbow, and then he gathered her next to him and they started toward the trail. Miserable, she hunched against him and let herself be led. She bit her lip against the sharp pain, which worked itself into a pulsing ache and made her dizzy. She must have badly sprained her wrist, or even broken it. The repercussions were more than she was ready to consider. She leaned heavily on Raleigh, and his support was more comforting than she expected.

Halfway up the trail, he stopped and swung her into his arms. When she would have protested, he merely frowned at her. Immediately the tears brimmed again, and she despised her helplessness. She wasn't used to this. It made Raleigh's strong arms around her all the more powerful, and unwittingly she resented him for her own weakness. He just held her all the closer until she couldn't hold back the tears. Her frustration found an outlet in anger, and he was the convenient target.

"Where were you? If you had come at four this wouldn't have happened."

"Naturally. I knew this was coming. I suppose I lured you up on onto the cliff, too."

"Well, if you hadn't scolded me I wouldn't have slipped. I was doing just fine."

"Of course you were."

She could have killed him. He silently walked up the slope, and she could see the serious set of his jaw. Her good arm was around his neck and she felt all twisted around. She knew she must be tiring him, and she was glad. She wished she were so heavy he'd have to put her down. At the same time she wasn't sure she could walk up by herself. She sniffed back the tears. Inconsiderate brute. He hadn't even said why he was late. She concentrated on staying mad in order to ignore her wrist.

Soon they reached the rim of the crater, and a few sure strides brought them to his car. He set her on her feet, and held the door for her while she sat down. Then he reached into the back for a stray newspaper. He folded it in half, and held it out in front of her. She instantly realized what he intended. Laying her wrist over "Street" of *The Wall Street Journal*, she watched him securely roll the paper around her wrist and lower arm. It was a crude splint, but it would help against the worst jerks of the road. She held it up with her free hand and looked up as he stepped away from her. It would have been a good time to thank him, but her wrist was hurting even more, and he was frowning again.

"What about my car?" she asked.

His frown deepened with annoyance.

"You can't drive. You may be stubborn and exasperating, but you're not stupid. Not usually, that is."

Instantly Claire bridled. She'd finally goaded his impatience, too.

"Of course not," she snapped. "I was just thinking if the ranger found my car he'd be worried."

Without a word, he ripped a piece of paper from her notepad and walked over to the Scout. He rolled up the windows and stuck the note on the dash. Coming back, he slammed Claire's door and walked around to the driver's side.

"What did you say on it?" she asked, relentless.

"I said you had been attacked and were never, ever coming back."

Claire stared out her window and allowed the fresh tears to slide down her cheeks. Raleigh drove out in silence, the Fiat moving smoothly under his capable hands. Next to him Claire made a deplorably ungrateful damsel in distress. Her newspapered wrist sat awkwardly in her lap, and she gripped the top of her arm where a scratch was seeping a slow trickle of blood into her shirt. She was wretchedly unhappy. The cold war going on in the car was a major contributor to her unhappiness, but she didn't know what to do about it so she just sat there, blinking at the window and wishing he would say something. Something not mean.

As they passed Stovepipe Wells, he gave her a sharp look that she felt rather than saw, and then he changed gears and kept going. It was another twenty miles to Furnace Creek, but the ranger station and any medical facilities would be there.

"How do you feel?" he asked, when she rested her head on the back of her seat and closed her eyes. Her face was drained of color. The newspaper slid down a little.

"Okay."

"It looks better than I thought at first."

"Thanks."

"I don't think anything's broken, but it's swelling up pretty badly."

She bit back a peevish comment about astute observations and tried to concentrate on the edge of the folddown window shade. He hadn't been concerned at first, no. He'd waited until she was recovering, and then he was Dr. Optimist himself. As if noticing how hard she had to try to contain herself, he suddenly smiled at her.

"At least it's your left hand."

"I'm left-handed," she said flatly.

In the following silence, the gravity of her situation hit her. The sprain itself was not that big a problem, but without the use of both hands, she couldn't drive. The camera was certainly out of commission. Her project would have to be put on hold for several days, maybe a week. That could be disastrous. She took a big breath and slowly let it out again. This was going to need some thinking over. The ending was so near, just a couple more sites. She could forgo the extra research she had wanted to add, and she could take a minimum of notes, but she had to at least complete her original proposal. There must be a way to continue it without having to put it off until she could drive. With increasing agitation, she realized she would have to call Harris for assistance or an extension. The very thought made her feel physically sick, and she wondered that her aversion to the absent man had already grown so much since lunchtime. Anxiously she lifted her wrist free from the newspaper and inspected the swelling. It simply couldn't be as bad as it felt.

"Hey. Be careful. The less you move it the better."

She rewrapped it and braced it high to slow the swelling. Her dread added to her sense of urgency.

"Are we almost there?" she asked.

He glanced at her and, misreading her worry for pain, he stepped on the accelerator. The Fiat raced toward Furnace Creek. Claire caught her breath and marveled at the speed. Being close to the ground made the miles go by even faster. It was just the release she needed, and by the time they arrived, her cheeks had regained their color and she felt decidedly better.

"I think it'll be all right if I get some ice on it for the rest of the day. I have an Ace bandage for later." The lowness of her voice made her sound more drained than she really was, and after a moment of hesitation she spoke more lightly.

"I want to thank you. I've been shrewish, I know, and I'm sorry. I was just angry at myself for falling and this will slow up my research, but I'll be okay."

It had been difficult to say, and the bit about the research was an understatement she hadn't thought she could pull off. It teased her tears.

"You're in the trailer park, right?"

Had he even heard her? She nodded, feeling numb, and they pulled up to her little trailer. With her hand balanced in the air, she gingerly opened her door and got out. Raleigh brought her gear and followed her to the door. She tried to say good-night there, but he took her key, opened the door and let her in.

"Unless you're feeling exceptionally prudish today, I'm coming in to set you up with some ice."

It would have been childish to make a fuss, so she directed him to the Baggies and soon he had one filled with cubes. It wasn't so bad letting someone help her, but she wasn't accustomed to it. The numbness of the cold immediately began to cut through the pain, and in relief she smiled up at him from her seat on the couch. He wasn't looking at her, but at the disarray of the trailer and, too tired to be embarrassed, she let her eyes follow his gaze. Yes, it was the usual mess. When he finally looked at her, his face was not quite a blank.

"You shouldn't have bothered to clean up for me," he said, and the humor in his voice was clear for the first time that day.

"How does the wrist feel?" he continued, when she made no attempt to defend her chaos. His concern calmed her, and she was beginning to expect his odd way of swinging around on emotions. It seemed she couldn't take him seriously, and then he'd say something calculated to confuse her irritation.

"It feels better," she said, without conviction. In fact she didn't feel much of anything but cold. He eased himself onto the couch next to her and gently lifted the ice. A large blue and green swell completely disfigured her narrow wrist and hand. He touched it carefully, turning her hand over and inspecting it closely, while water from the ice bag dripped silently onto the floor. He stood up abruptly and handed back the cold bag.

"Yes, I think the ice will do the trick." His voice was oddly thick, and she looked up to see what had disturbed him. He turned however, and his profile was inscrutable. He took the few short steps to the back of the trailer in the beginning of a pace, but when he came to the darkroom door, he hesitated and looked back as if to ask if she minded. She gave a curt nod. He swung open the door and after a brief look around, he came back, surprised.

"I didn't realize you really used that camera. That's quite a setup back there." He left the comment hanging.

Claire knew it was an invitation to discuss her photography, and if the opportunity had come at a different time, she would have had quite a bit to say. As it was, she was catching a peculiar shyness and her mind was too full of her present predicament. Raleigh saw her hesitation.

"You don't need to talk to me about it if you'd rather not. It's just that I'm interested in photography too, and I must admit it's unusual to find a complete darkroom in the back of a trailer—particularly one that's so small you can't even stand up straight."

He smiled, daring her to take offense, and she knew she was being charmed. She was not immune to it. It was dangerous to have him showing a real interest in her. She would have to watch herself, she thought. Raleigh could be more than attractive when he chose to let down his guard. Between her exhaustion and the unexpected attention, her mind went blank except for the phrase "You're a pro," and that would never do.

He was watching her, leaning against the little kitchen counter, with his arms folded and his head nearly touching the ceiling. He shifted. She didn't know what he was doing here still.

"The conspicuous topic seems to strike out again," he said, and rolled his shoulders as if the space were indeed beginning to cramp him.

How could she be so outstandingly slow-witted? She was aware that the intangible tension was creeping between them again, now that her injury was no longer the top concern. The silence was thick with potential communication, and only put her more on edge. Anything she might have said couldn't fill the pause, but her expression must have told him something. He smiled and moved forward, and opened the door.

"You're a minx," he said. "You lure me into your trailer, and then let me look the fool while you sit there, smug."

She was stunned. He had misunderstood entirely.

"Well, of all the nerve! I'm sitting here with a broken wrist and you expect me to entertain you. What do you think this is?"

Raleigh laughed, and she got to watch the mirth in his eyes spread to his whole face. She wasn't disappointed. He pocketed his hands and leaned against the door frame, and she perceived that he had baited her once again. Only this time she didn't feel he was mocking her, and instead they laughed together. The tension vanished, and the pause that followed was even more intimate than the first. Claire readjusted her ice, and when she looked up again, she was blushing lightly. Their eyes held, as if they were both startled by something and wanted to see if the other had noticed it too. Raleigh straightened, and then stepped backward out of the trailer, steadying himself with a hand on the door handle. He looked back at Claire.

"Since you don't need any more assistance—" he stopped as his words reminded him of something "—and since I don't need to alert the ranger, I'd better go."

With him standing outside and her seated on the couch, their eyes were on a level, but she noticed he now avoided meeting her glance.

"Maybe I could help you out tomorrow. Since you can't drive and I'd like to do some sightseeing, maybe I could give you a lift and see some of the Valley at the same time." He fiddled the door handle back and forth.

Claire wasn't sure. The chances that they wanted to go to the same places were slim, but on the other hand they had already met in some unlikely spots, and she certainly couldn't do her work on her own. She hadn't expected him to grasp the full significance of her injury and now she admitted she should have given him credit. This unusual man was really too much, standing there nonchalantly in the doorway. You'd think he expected to be turned down. It made her want to laugh. She smiled.

"If you're sure you wouldn't mind, that would help a lot."

He nodded, keeping his face serious, and dug for his keys.

"Fine. What's a good time?"

She thought for a second. She was used to being up early, but she wasn't sure how much she could impose.

"Eight," he supplied. "We can have breakfast after we've gotten someplace."

He must have read her mind. That settled it. He was gone from the rectangle of the doorway, and in a minute the Fiat was turning the corner.

Claire leaned back against her couch. She moved the ice to a better position on her wrist and closed her eyes. Oh, Raleigh. For a moment her mind was so full she couldn't think, and then different images flashed from her memory. He had been so gentle, and so changing. He had been gruff, and then like a kid; nothing like the sophisticated man at the party the night before. Was this the side of him Sophie knew? Why had he volunteered to help her out tomorrow, and why did she feel slightly short of breath at the idea? She was drained, yet excited at the same time. She sat up again. He had felt something too, she was sure. For a second there, she had almost expected him to kiss her goodbye; but that was absurd.

Steadying herself in more ways than one, she got up and found an extra bag for the leaky ice. She took a couple of aspirins and settled in for a slow evening. As she lay down again, she smiled to herself, remembering his unexpected laughter. It really was something. Maybe he would smile like that the next day. She chuckled at herself.

"You're in for it now, Claire," she said to the gathering dusk.

## *Chapter Five*

Raleigh was prompt, to Claire's discomposure.

She had trouble waking, as usual, and found it hard to believe it was actually morning when her alarm went off. She would have rolled over and fallen asleep again but a corner of sunlight snuck through the curtains with nagging persistence until she remembered. Raleigh. She was still brushing the sleepy tangles from her hair when she heard him striding across the gravel toward her trailer, and throwing down the brush, she opened the door before he could knock. He paused in midpace, looking at her slender figure in the doorway. The morning discovered her slightly disarrayed, but graceful just the same. She wore jeans and an oversize lemon-yellow shirt; distinctly comfortable and practical. Her bandaged wrist made the only awkward angle, and Raleigh hardly noticed it. He was clad in khaki trousers and a short-sleeved cotton shirt in a riveting shade of blue. His light eyes scanned her as if they had never met before, and then he smiled. Claire gave an answering smile, and when the bright sun glinted into her eyes, she had a strong desire to chuckle.

"Good morning," he said. "You don't look like you're about to do murder, so your wrist must be better." Before she could deny ever having any violent tendencies, he made a quarter turn and called over his shoulder.

"Thanks, Frank."

A man on the edge of the parking lot waved and started up the road, and Claire was startled to see her Scout parked quietly behind her trailer. She blinked. After all, it was still early; but no, it really was there. She stared at Raleigh, already suspecting something unpleasant, and the question puckered itself on her face.

"I thought we'd bring your car back for you," he volunteered.

He slid his hands into his trousers, clearly pleased with himself, and distractingly attractive.

"But you don't have the keys," she began, feeling manipulated rather than grateful. What was he doing, taking care of her business? She had spent from three A.M. until four A.M. contriving an elaborate and tedious plan for getting the Scout back, and her relief at not needing to execute it was equal to her annoyance at him for interfering.

"How did you get it here?" she insisted.

He had the grace to look slightly abashed, but not for long. His voice was far from conciliatory. In fact, the brag was barely concealed.

"I left one of the doors unlocked yesterday when I saw you had left nothing valuable inside. I used to hot-wire my brother's jeep all the time when I was a kid. Yours was a cinch." He was strolling toward her as he talked.

"I didn't think you'd mind. If you like, I'll get Frank to drive it back to Ubehebe."

"You're too much," she said, giving in. The bold lout. She hadn't been consulted, he had acted most improperly, and yet the result would save her a deal of trouble, and she knew he knew she knew it. Besides, his grin made quibbling impossible.

She smiled back at him. He seemed to think he could move her and her car around at will, but it was partly her own fault for having let him drive her home the night before. Let someone help you oncc, and they think they can do anything for you. She would have to straighten him out about it sometime.

Raleigh watched her thinking, and approved of what he saw. He propelled her along by asking if she was ready to go.

"Just a second. I have some things for breakfast." She popped back inside the trailer and grabbed a brown grocery bag and her knapsack. She passed them to Raleigh, who carried them to his car, and within minutes the two of them were heading through town. As they passed Jolly's Date Stand under the palms, Claire saw the little round face look over a customer's shoulder to watch them go by. She was about to wave, when Jolly turned quickly back to her business. For an instant Claire was puzzled, and then wondered if Jolly hadn't recognized her.

Raleigh had seen the direction of her glance, and as they pulled into the open road, he looked over at her.

"Did you want some dates?"

"No, it's just that—" She stopped. "I just thought it looked cool there under the palms."

He laughed, a comfortable grumble over the engine's hum.

"You couldn't be hot already. This is the only cool time of the day."

Claire warmed to his good mood, shaking off the last chill of Jolly's movement. Settling into her low seat and resting her Ace-bandaged wrist in her lap, she closed her eyes and grinned. She hadn't been in a fast car for ages, and she hadn't been able to enjoy it properly the day before. She could feel the land whipping past her and she knew, quite frankly, that she loved it.

"Where are we going, anyway?" she asked, without opening her eyes.

"When you ease up on your work you really go whole hog, don't you?"

That got her to open her eyes.

"What do you mean?"

"I could be heading for Las Vegas, for all you know, and ten minutes later you casually remember to wonder where we're going."

"We can't go to Las Vegas."

He laughed.

"That's just what I mean. When you put away the shrewd geologist you're just another gullible—"

"Stop right there," she interrupted, violet eyes glittering dangerously. "If we're going to get along at all, you can stuff—I beg your pardon. I mean, if we're going to get along, I'd prefer that you didn't make any comments like the one that promised to be."

"Christ." He laughed again. "You're almost as touchy as I am. I only hope we don't murder each other before we get back to Furnace Creek."

There didn't seem to be anything to say to that, and Claire watched apprehensively for a second before realizing he didn't intend to turn around right there. Maybe she was a little gullible. They drove in silence for a while and though he still hadn't said where they were going, she didn't want to ask again. He must have read her mind.

"Have you been to Dante's View yet?"

Delight quickened her pulse.

"No, I haven't. I've been meaning to go, but I kept putting it off. You know how it is. I don't really need to do anything up there. I was hoping to have time before I left. It's supposed to be a spectacular view."

"It is. How soon are you leaving?"

"That depends. In a few days, maybe."

They took a turn off the main road, and began climbing steadily on long, winding curves. The road got rougher and narrower, and she noticed the Fiat had no trouble handling it. She had thought racy little cars were only good for speed, but she had to admit her Scout couldn't have performed better.

Soon they reached the summit, and as soon as the engine quieted, they could hear the wind. Silently, Claire stepped out and was instantly swept back by a burst of air.

"Isn't this great?" she called.

Her hair became a joke with that first gust, and she reached back into the car for her sweater. Then she was drawn impulsively toward the very edge of the cliff. It was the most beautiful sight she had ever seen. The distance and space were more than striking. Below, to her left, stretched the length of Death Valley. The drop of five thousand feet changed the meandering streams into mere threads of reflected sunlight. Opposite ran the Panamint range, and beyond, to the west, were more and more lines of mountains fading into the pale of the sky for as far as she could see. Grays, blues, browns and violets spread endlessly below an arc of blue, where only the faintest of clouds pulled the eye even higher. She stood spellbound, stirred by a vague longing and forgetting everything but the magnificence before her.

The sound of a door slam made her turn. Raleigh had only now left the car, and she was secretly grateful that he hadn't intruded.

"Can you believe this?" she asked.

It had struck him too, she could tell. His face was composed as he joined her, while his arms were spilling over with a blanket, the breakfast things she had packed and a basket she hadn't seen yet. He made a curious sight, and she smiled. Together they walked along the path on the ridge, and almost immediately they ran across a forestry sign.

"'Quite a view, isn't it—serene, quiet, eternal,'" he read aloud. "I guess they don't want us to miss anything."

She appreciated the glint in his blue eyes. They stepped nearer to the cliff, finding a ledge out of the wind and a smooth rock to sit on. For a moment they just looked down at the valley. Corny as it was, the sign had been right. There was something eternal about the valley stretching below them, gleaming in the morning light and shrouded in the silence of the wind. There were no trees, only clumps of grasses in the rock. A stray breeze slipped under her collar and made her shiver. She was aware of feeling vulnerable—perhaps the rawness was infectious—and she self-consciously turned to look at Raleigh. He was frowning at Telescope Peak, the highest point in the Panamints, and he was unaware of her gaze.

She studied his profile: straight, strong-chinned. A dark lock of hair swept over his eyebrows, and another begged her to tuck it behind his ear. What other women had seen him like this? So many secrets behind his guard. There was vulnerability under his changing toughness, a pensiveness he hadn't shown her before, and she was drawn to him even more, in a new way. What peculiar chance had brought them to Dante's View together? This morning, for the first time, the tension between them had eased into something comfortable, yet it was still pregnant with unasked questions. Did he feel it too? She resolved to relish the compatibility of the moment, in case it was a one-sided illusion, and so she was almost sorry when Raleigh shook out of his mood and turned to her. For just an instant, a question lingered in his penetrating eyes; then he slid, ever so subtly, back into the man who dealt with his world. She was effectively pushed to a less intimate distance.

She was still absorbing the changes in him when he spoke.

"You must be starved by now, even though it is quite a view. I am. Let's see what we have here."

He spread out the blanket, and began opening the basket he had brought. Claire watched with growing amusement as he pulled out yogurt, apples, a small jar of preserves and, finally, a small loaf of homemade bread. When he reached in for two plastic knives and napkins, his face said "smug" all over it. She kept her smile to herself, and one by one, pulled an identical assortment of food out of her own paper bag, except her jam was date rather than strawberry. He took a long look at the doubles of everything and leaned his head back and howled. She laughed with him.

"We should have known, of course. There's only one place to buy groceries for fifty miles, but even so, it's funny we picked the same things," she said.

"'Funny' is hardly the word for it. It's hilarious. If we'd tried, we couldn't have matched up more closely. You know what it is?" His voice dropped. "I say we give the credit to Dante, or better yet, we'll give it to the desert magic. We'll be lucky if it's not all poisoned. You know about the magic, don't you? They say it makes good things better and bad things worse, and tricks you up sometimes so you can't tell the difference."

"I like that," she said, not believing a word of it.

He shook his head, but he was smiling, too. She put her things back in the bag, and together they ate what Raleigh had brought. Picnics have a way of bringing out the kid in people, and the magic nonsense had already been a good start. The conversation took off in twenty directions at once, finally coming back to hot-wiring cars.

"Your brother must have been just as annoyed as I was when you did it to his jeep," she said.

Again Raleigh withdrew, and he paused before replying. Claire was puzzled. His eyes looked through her to something in his past, and instantly she realized she had touched a nerve. Impulsively, she reached her hand out and rested it on his arm. He was surprised, and she gently took her hand away. He shook his head and smiled again, but his voice showed he was slightly troubled.

"I've been thinking of him so much more than usual these days. My brother was, well, he absolutely devoured life. Everything was an intense game to him, and he loved it." He paused. "Yes, he got pretty mad a few times. He was a kid then." He narrowed his eyes on the severe lines of Telescope Peak once again. "He was killed a couple of years after that."

The last sentence was dry, but she could sense his bitterness. She knew the little he'd told her was the beginning of an iceberg, and she waited, but nothing more came. She didn't want to push him, so she began speaking gently.

"I have a brother. Thomas. He lives in London now, with his wife. We lived with my uncle in Chicago when our parents died, and I adored him, fiercely. I suppose I drove him crazy at times. He keeps insisting I come over and visit them, but it depends on how this project works out." The thought of it geared her mind around to her business of the day, and a little butterfly of nerves reminded her she had a lot to do still. Raleigh had come around again, taking the step out of his train of thought into the action of the moment. It was as if, even as absorbing as they were, he could put away his memories like an old friend he could meet up with again later. His slow grin assured her that he knew this was all very well, but she had pressing things to do. He tossed an apple core into the basket.

"I can see your mind working. Just name the place, and we'll get going to your first site."

Relieved, she smiled at him, and together they gathered their things and headed back to the car. With the door slamming out the wind, the air in the car was especially still, and the top of the mountain looked like the backdrop for a silent movie. Something had happened to them here. She tucked her loose hair behind her ear and tentatively touched her wrist. It throbbed a warning. She would have to take it easy.

Claire had thought the night before about the few sites she had left to visit, cutting them down to the two most essential. She knew at least one of them, and probably both, would not be particularly interesting to Raleigh. She hadn't been sure which place to visit first, but had finally decided on the more dramatic one. Maybe that way he wouldn't get bored and his chauffeuring would last longer.

"Do you know Titus Canyon?" she asked.

"No."

She turned and recognized the grim line of his tightened jaw. He was thinking again, inaccessible; and she wondered what could be troubling him. He was exasperating, really.

"It's amazing," she began, summoning an effort to divert him. "A cavern cuts between two canyon walls, scraped deep by the runoff from the surrounding hills. You don't want to be anywhere near it when the flash floods come because the water reaches maybe twenty feet up the walls, and anything alive wouldn't stand a chance."

"I hadn't planned on being there in the rain."

Or any other time, she thought. What had gotten into him?

"If you'd rather not start there, I need to go to Salt Creek. That's closer."

"Salt Creek," he repeated, his voice deceptively mild. "I bet that's a creek with salt in it. Quite a thrill, maybe. Look, I don't mind driving you, but I think we'd better strike a deal. For each place I take you, why don't you come with me somewhere I'd like to go too? That way I can get in some sightseeing between the geology lessons."

He'd done it again. She was baffled. He didn't need to drive her around at all. If it was such a problem, he'd want to keep it down to a minimum, in any case; but it sounded as if he were intending to spend more than a little time with her. It could be intense time, too, and he underestimated how interesting she could make the geology. It would be fun, even; and she secretly vowed to make him swallow his snide attitude toward her work. She looked out the window as a sliver of anticipation lifted her heart. One of these days she was going to take a closer look at what this man was doing to her feelings, but for the moment she rose to the challenge.

"You mustn't let me impose on you," she said meekly.

He grimaced, and harmony was restored. The deal was struck, and they headed on to Titus Canyon, leaving Salt Creek for the next day.

The settling of the routine was a load off Claire's mind.

"I won't have to call Harris," she muttered, unaware that she was thinking aloud. She hadn't known how much this possibility had bothered her until it was eliminated, and now she felt relief and a corner of real gratitude toward Raleigh. He was beginning to take on the proportions of a benevolent wizard—between retrieving her car and warding off Harris. She would have to thank him properly.

"Look out the back," he said, peering at his rearview mirror.

Curious, she shifted carefully around in her seat, and far back down the valley she saw a fog that swirled into an opaque gray cloud even as she watched.

"A sandstorm."

"And that's not all," he said, pointing off to his left.

The weather had decided to perform for them. To the west, it snowed upon the Cottonwood Mountains. To the east, it alternately snowed and rained into the Grapevines. And directly above them a blue sky loomed,

oblivious to everything else. Claire had never seen such
a combination. She watched, enthralled, as Raleigh
steered the car down the highway toward Titus Canyon.
When they finally pulled up on the gravel, she was still
exhilarated by the power of the sandstorm. Sandstorms
simply hadn't made it to Chicago yet, and the new experience had awed her for the second time in a day. Raleigh couldn't help noticing.

"Spellbound again, aren't you? I don't know whether
it's your gullibility—" he emphasized the word "—or
the magic of the desert itself."

"Well," she retorted, "it couldn't possibly be my
gullibility, so we'll have to chalk up another one to the
magic."

He had no objections. They got out and started up the
canyon, he carrying her light sack. They went up the
gravel and around a bend, and the walls shot up on
either side of them, cutting the horizon to a line of blue
way above them. Their footsteps echoed off the bright
stone and the next bend beckoned them on.

"This must be my day," she murmured to herself. The
canyon was one of her favorite places, and suddenly she
wasn't sure if she was ready to share it. Would Raleigh
appreciate it as she did? She would hate to spoil it by
having his view of it jar with her own. Looking at him
she decided to take a chance. As they walked, she
launched into an explanation of the various strata in the
canyon walls, pointing out the different smoothnesses
where water had churned against the softer stone.
Warming to her favorite topic, she was unaware that she
herself was breathing drama into the lifeless marble. He
kept up with her, occasionally asking an intelligent
question, and finally he wandered off by himself when
she sat down to take some notes.

He came back just as she was finishing, and swung her sack lightly over his shoulder. His cotton shirt was damp, and a patch of tan chest showed where the windless heat had made him loosen another button. He looked thoughtful rather than bored.

"So what do you think?" she asked.

He took another gaze up to the tops of the cliffs, and looked back at her upturned face. The streaked stone behind her almost matched the auburn of her hair, and the rock held potential strength that lay dormant in her as well. Surprised by his own thoughts, he reached down quickly for a flat stone. With a half turn he pitched it up the distance to the next bend, where it skipped against another before landing out of sight.

"See that?" he began. His voice was low, but it filled the silence. "My first thought was that I had to go back for my camera, but then I realized this is the kind of place you can't photograph. Perhaps a painter could capture some of this in an abstract composition, but I couldn't. I would lose it. See that vertical, there, and there? I'm not sure how to say what I mean. A photo wouldn't do it justice. It would be just a picture, a copy. Empty." He lowered his arm, but left his gaze on the cliffs, and his voice dropped to a hush. "I'll just have to remember."

His enthusiasm had reached straight through to his core and brought out this. She instinctively respected it for what it was, and marveled that the man had a bit of poet in him. He hadn't spoiled her canyon at all. Instead, he had given her a perspective that would make her own memories all the more vivid.

He shrugged, and grinned at her, taking a step toward the way out.

"How's the wrist?"

"It's all right," she said, raising her voice over the noise of their feet in the pebbles. "In fact, it's my right that's getting worn-out. When I was a kid, they taught me to write with my right hand before they figured out I was a lefty, so it's not as if I'd never tried before. But almost! The notes come pretty slowly."

They walked down the canyon, winding quickly around the bends until they reached the final one. They had just been laughing again when he put a hand on her arm and she turned, mildly surprised.

He was looking at her, blue eyes searching hers, and he was about to say something. After an eternity he still didn't speak, and Claire felt a butterfly stirring inside her.

"What is it?" she asked softly.

Far off, a roll of thunder mumbled and Raleigh reached a long finger toward her cheek, following the smooth line down to her chin in a gentle caress. His eyes lingered on her face in a way that shone with something entirely new, and her skin felt the flicker of a thrill under his touch. A strand of copper hair brushed the back of his hand when at last he moved it away. Expectant, she watched as again he tried to speak, and then changed his mind.

"I just—nothing. Nothing, really. I need to get back. An appointment." His manner shifted as he moved away from her, and disappointment lurched unbidden in her throat.

What was he doing? What had he wanted to say? She was puzzled and not a little vexed. Could this possibly be the same man who had ruthlessly kissed her in Shoshone? It didn't fit at all. She bit back her curiosity. She wanted to respect his reticence, but wanted just as badly to know what was going through his mind. Could

it have been something about the canyon or her wrist or
the weather? Hardly. She knew it had been something
more, and of a quite different nature, and she knew just
as clearly that he had decided not to tell her. Exasperating. Try as she might, she couldn't help feeling hurt.
Somehow his intimate touch was even more violating
than that rough kiss had been. Had their growing
friendship and trust been an illusion, a trick of the desert? Driving back beside him in uncomfortable silence,
she could believe it was. Hadn't he even warned her, in
a way? She became steadily more blue, and on top of it,
her wrist was aching more than it had all day. From deep
inside, her anger began to boil. What did he think he was
doing? Well, she thought, if he wasn't going to explain
himself, she certainly wasn't going to give him the pleasure of asking him what was going on. She fumed, gently
at first, and then with gusto, all the way back to Furnace Creek. He could just keep his crazy moods and
treacherous signals to himself.

"Where are you taking me?" she asked involun-
tarily. "That was my turn."

"There's a book I want to lend you. Ansel Adams
took some amazing photos in Zion National Park, and
the canyon reminded me of them. I thought you'd like
to see them."

What? Claire was stunned, and not particularly
pleased. She didn't want to be in his debt any more than
she already was. Even more, she didn't like the way he
assumed she'd want his book, and then hauled her off
with him to pick it up. He might at least ask her. She resisted a childish impulse to insist he drop her off, summoning her dignity. Next to her, Raleigh registered her
stiff expression and his jaw set with a determination of
his own. The car sped along with two slumbering vol-

canos perched precariously inside, and when they reached the hotel and stepped out, there was relief on both their faces. Another moment, and they would have been laughing about it together, clearing the air, but just then they were interrupted by a peal of laughter, and they looked up.

Sophie Blake was sitting at a table at the edge of the terrace and she beckoned to them. Across from her, Jake Bowing smiled at them just over his shoulder.

"Just the very people we were discussing. Come up and join us before you melt out there. You look exhausted!"

Claire groaned inwardly and shot a beseeching glance at Raleigh. He wasn't looking at her, but was smiling instead at Sophie. The parking lot was hot and breezeless, and Jake took a long swallow from an icy glass. Without hesitation, Raleigh called back.

"We'll be right up."

"Raleigh, I can't," Claire whispered urgently.

He looked at her then, surprised and skeptical. Coming as it did, it would be inexplicably rude to refuse Sophie's invitation. Even so, Claire was giving it a try. The last thing she wanted to do was to be social and polite.

"You look fine," he said flatly, slamming the car door. She blushed. He had misunderstood.

They walked up the shallow steps into the coolness of the lobby and then through the French doors onto the terrace. It was hot here, too, with midafternoon brightness, but at least there was a little wind, and a cool pitcher of water stood on every table. Several of the tables were occupied, one by a couple intent over their chessboard.

Claire absorbed this as they strolled over to Sophie and Jake. Sophie was wearing a delicate straw hat, a sleeveless white blouse and a pleated white linen skirt. She had taken her feet out of her sandals and her legs disappeared under the tablecloth. She looked cool, and happy, and genuinely appealing. The simple clothes were cut to reveal her figure, and the white set off the rich tones of her skin. The shadow cast by the wide brim of her hat dappled her face with points of sunlight, and her green, heavy-lidded eyes looked up with a mix of innocence and mischief. The color of laughter brightened her face as her previous makeup hadn't, and Claire decided, critically, that she was a stunning woman. Any man would be a fool not to think so. Raleigh was shaking his head at her, smiling.

"You make a charming bohemian," he said. There was a gleam of mockery in the corner of his eye.

Claire experienced a sinking sensation, and Sophie's laughter welled up again.

"You're a toad, Ral. Knock him down for me, Jake."

Jake was leaning back in his chair, nursing an iced tea in both hands. He shook his blond head and chuckled.

"No, no," Jake corrected. "He said 'charming,' Sophie, not 'alarming.' Can't knock him down for that."

The three of them laughed. Claire had followed it, but she felt she had missed something. She smiled, but she knew she only looked stiff. She was acutely conscious of the other guests on the terrace, and she knew her grubby attire was drawing their curious glances. What was she doing here? She tried to catch Raleigh's eye, but he had leaned away to borrow a chair from the next table. Now he held it for her, placing it on Jake's right, and there was nothing to do but sit down and make the best of it. She hitched her loose yellow shirt straight on her shoulders and passed a hand over her hair.

"I'll be right back down," Raleigh said. "I have to get a book for Claire. Order me one of those, won't you?" he added, nodding toward Jake's glass. Then he was gone.

As Sophie's eyes settled on her for the first time, Claire got the distinct impression she'd been left to the wolves.

## Chapter Six

Nervous energy was gathering in Claire's knees and elbows, and though she'd been nearly exhausted a few minutes before, now she itched to be moving. It took a good deal of self-control not to fidget in her chair. She crossed one dusty knee over the other and was thankful her tennis shoes were under the table. Small comforts.

Sophie leaned forward and slid a package of cigarettes and a lighter off the white tablecloth. She offered them with a shrugged shoulder, but Jake and Claire both declined.

"How it can be so hot in March I have absolutely no idea," Sophie began. She spoke in a steady stream as she shook out a cigarette and lit up, and the first puff circled her hat before dissipating into the air. Claire didn't follow what she was saying. She was distracted by the movements of Sophie's graceful hands and the threads of smoke, and she was hoping Raleigh would hurry. A silence grew longer, and Claire pulled at her wits. Sophie was smiling expectantly.

"I'm sorry, what did you say?" Claire asked.

Sophie's smile deepened.

"I asked about your wrist. It must be awfully inconvenient not being able to write or drive or anything."

"It is," she answered bluntly.

"Fortunately, you're nearly finished, aren't you?"

Claire almost laughed.

"Yes, I am. I should be here only a couple more days, and then I'll pack my things and go."

There was no point hedging. She knew what Sophie wanted to hear. Her charming appearance might beguile Jake and Raleigh, but Claire was not deceived. Underneath, Sophie was calculating and devious enough for twenty jealous wives.

The iced tea arrived, and the waiter filled the glasses, Jake's and Sophie's as well. Claire gratefully took a swallow, and then set the glass back on the table, where drops quickly began to bead on the outside, despite the dry wind.

Sophie wore a contemplative expression.

"Don't you think it would have been better if you'd sprained your ankle?" she asked.

"I hadn't thought of it."

Sophie tapped her cigarette against the tray and continued lightly, explaining.

"Well, then you'd still be able to write and everything, but you'd still need someone to help with the driving."

"I don't think I understand you," Claire said carefully. In fact, she was getting an idea, and she didn't like it.

Sophie laughed, and made a generous, all-encompassing sweep with her hand.

"Oh, come on," she said, even more lightly. "You're among friends. I'm not above a little deceit myself now and then, when it's harmless and it serves my purpose. I merely suggest that I would have sprained my ankle instead."

A tense moment elapsed, and then Claire drew herself up perfectly straight. She summoned infinite poise and pride, and glared coolly at Sophie, while inside she seethed at the insult. As if she would ever stoop to such a conniving manipulation!

"No doubt you would have," she answered deliberately.

She rose in order to leave, but Jake reached to detain her, and quickly intervened.

"No, wait. She didn't mean that. Of course we know you had an accident. It is extremely unfortunate, and she only means to say that, to say that—"

He stopped, prompting Sophie, but Sophie merely leaned back and extended her cigarette toward the ashtray. Her heavy-lidded eyes pointedly avoiding meeting Claire's.

"Sophie!" Jake exclaimed. It was a demand.

"Oh, it's too hot to disagree," Sophie murmured. "Jake's right. Of course I meant nothing."

In a rat's hole. Claire had the urge to deliver a concise, scathing remark, but Raleigh chose that moment to reappear. She yielded to Jake's pleading gaze, and sank quietly back into her seat. By the time Raleigh reached the table, Sophie was laughing easily, as if nothing had happened, and Jake took his cue from her.

Raleigh set a slim hardcover book at Claire's elbow and reached for his glass.

"I'm dry as toast," he said, taking a swallow.

He seemed larger, standing there with the glass tipped to his lips. He positioned another chair between Claire's and Sophie's, and he flicked the brim of Sophie's hat as he sat down. The gesture spoke volumes about familiarity, and Claire felt something go soft in her stomach.

"What did you do with yourself anyway, all day long?" he asked Sophie.

She adjusted her shoulders so that she was closer to Raleigh than the chairs had initially dictated. He seemed unaware of it.

"It's been so hot," she said, and the last word came out like a lazy salamander from a rock. "Everyone else went off to the pool but I knew it would be a zoo there. Any vagabond in town can get in. Then they positively sit in the water until the layers wash off. It's a health hazard."

"Come on," Jake laughed. "It's not that bad. Having a few of the townspeople adds variety to the crowd."

Sophie sniffed.

"You're entitled to whatever you think, of course."

Raleigh and Jake laughed, exchanging glances.

"Poor little bohemian," Raleigh said. "She wants the pool to herself and everyone else can just go swim in the salt flats."

"Well now, I wouldn't go that far," Sophie conceded. "They can have the par-four pond on the golf course. George would rather be there anyway."

That led them to discuss Sophie's other guests, and Claire was effectively excluded from the conversation. The best she could do was to try to smile at the right moments. It was hopeless. She felt awkward and stupid now, too, on top of underdressed and dusty. Why couldn't Raleigh have dropped her off at home instead of dragging her along, showing her just how badly she fit in his world? For this was unquestionably his world.

"But that's what I'm saying," Sophie argued. "If he hadn't redone the bathroom in beige and salmon she never would have divorced him."

Raleigh laughed and shook his head at her again.

Sophie continued smoothly on. At one point she leaned forward, for effect, and assured herself of Raleigh's attention by lightly touching his hand. Her hand rested a moment too long, and he didn't seem to notice. He and Sophie had a connection their body language couldn't deny, and Claire was the unwilling witness.

"How did that show for the handicapped go?" she asked Jake abruptly.

She simply couldn't sit like a vegetable any longer, and she had taken a sudden dislike to both Sophie and Raleigh.

"Nice of you to remember," Jake answered.

He began to tell about it. Sophie didn't wait for him to finish, but spoke softly to Raleigh on the side. Two conversations were deftly created, and Sophie had Raleigh all to herself. At first, Claire listened attentively to Jake, determined to ignore the other conversation, but it was impossible not to be aware of Raleigh. He'd given his ear to Sophie, but his pensive frown was directed at Claire, and she became increasingly self-conscious. What was he watching? Why did he so jealously follow the way she sipped her iced tea? He must be seeing her through Sophie's eyes, all dusty and awkward, and a blush stole up her face. She tried all the harder to devote her attention to Jake, and Jake was not immune to her encouraging smiles. Raleigh frowned even more.

She was being stretched thinner and thinner. Jake's smiles, Raleigh's frown and Sophie's clear, persistent voice were pulling her in different directions, bombarding her with conflicting demands. She tried in vain to collect herself. She took another taste of the iced tea, and spilled a slosh of liquid as she set the glass back on the table.

Sophie stopped talking in surprise, and her look of false concern was more than Claire could bear. She scraped her chair back and reached for the book Raleigh had brought down. Then she stood and automatically tapped her pockets in the habit she had when wearing her geology clothes. It was a series of jerky movements, and Sophie's eyes widened. Jake leaned forward to put a hand on the arm of Claire's chair.

"Are you feeling all right?" Jake asked.

Raleigh said nothing, watching her closely.

"I'm fine, I'm fine," she said hurriedly. Jake was even more concerned. "I just need to get home, that's all."

Too late she realized how peculiar her behavior was. There was a silence around the table, and then Jake stood up.

"Well, let me give you a lift," he offered. "I was about to head off myself."

She knew this wasn't true. Everyone else had been perfectly comfortable, and she felt keenly responsible for disrupting the party. But she'd been shattering inside, and now she wanted desperately to be away from there. Raleigh was standing too, and if anything, he looked a little bored. In a calmer state of mind, Claire would have recognized his detachment as a screen for something more.

"That's all right, Jake," he said. "Her things are in my car. I can take her back."

Claire blushed. He sounded as if she were an unpleasant responsibility of his. A nuisance. She recoiled at the thought.

"No, really, you don't have to get up. I can walk. It's not far. I'll be there in five minutes."

She searched anxiously around her. Jake was looking at her, smiling to indicate his offer was still good, but even he was puzzled by her behavior.

"Don't be silly, dear. You'd bake out there," came Sophie's calm voice from the table. "Ral, let her go with Jake."

She could have died. Raleigh's face darkened and his jaw set in a stubborn line.

"I'm taking her," he said. "If she's ready to go."

He took Claire's elbow and turned her toward the door without waiting for a reply. Jake sat down again, grinning, and Claire stuttered out a belated thanks. Sophie murmured goodbye, her face a pleasant mask. In an instant, Raleigh had bustled her out the door and through the lobby. She wrenched her arm free and glared at him. He merely held the door open for her and waited for her to go down the steps.

"How dare you!" she exclaimed.

"How dare I what?" he asked softly. His face was politely questioning, impeccably aloof. The open door compelled her to move forward, while he waited in expectant silence.

How dare he what! Of all the overbearing, high-handed, managing—! She couldn't believe him. It wasn't that he wanted to give her a lift, or even that he was concerned about her walking in the heat. He just hated to be crossed, and he couldn't let Jake or even Sophie outmaneuver him. Her elbow stung from his touch, as they sped down the road. His profile was devoid of all emotion. Inconsiderate, oblivious, intolerable, controlling—! The properly quelling description didn't exist. He and Sophie. They were a rotten pair, deserving of each other. Her throat tightened. She'd swallow her tongue before she gave him the satisfaction of seeing her vent her anger. She winced at the memory of her own graceless behavior, and lifted her chin a gulp higher.

This was a horrible way to end their day.

As they pulled into the trailer park, she checked her watch and realized it was after four. They had forgotten lunch, and knowing she was hungry added to her distress. She stepped out of the car and tried to get her sack out of the back before he could get out to help her. She succeeded in wrenching her wrist and behaving like a clod. When he came over to help her, she could happily have scratched his face.

"What's gotten into you?" he asked, flipping the seat forward and reaching in easily for her things.

*Into me?* she thought. *That's a good one.* She walked ahead and fit her key in the trailer door. She stepped in and reached out with her good hand. He handed her the sack and watched her settle it on the floor under the table. She maintained a chilly silence during the whole proceedings, and, to her utter amazement, amusement crept into his eyes when she reached stubbornly for the grocery bag. Teasing, he held it back.

"Well?"

"It's nothing," she snapped. "Just hand over my things."

The humor vanished and his face was stern.

"Now what's going on? I drive you back from Titus Canyon and you're a tomb the whole trip, then you throw Jake in my face and act like I have lice, and then you bite my head off for who-knows-what reason. I swear, Claire, I can't make heads or tails out of you."

He shoved the bag around the door and onto the table, then started walking away.

"Me?" she said shrilly. "I'm the tomb? That's terrific, coming from you."

He spun around.

"What's that supposed to mean?" he asked quietly.

Suddenly the tension sparked between them again, and if she had paused, she would have known she was on dangerous ground. She was too angry to back off, however, and lowering her voice, she let go.

"You're the one with all the secrets. I don't even know what you're doing in Death Valley. Even when you do start to say something, you clam up. It's as if you don't trust yourself. And then touching me like you did this afternoon; what was that? And that's just a beginning. First you have all the time in the world to drive me around, when I didn't even ask—and don't get me wrong, I appreciate it—but then you have appointments that pop out of nowhere; mighty convenient. And do you go to them? No. You drag me onto the terrace to try to be social to your friends. You knew how embarrassed I'd be. God. I was dressed wrong, I was dusty. I was exhausted and my wrist hurt, and now you're making me complain. Tomb!"

"You didn't like having Jake see you that way, did you?" he interjected smoothly.

She was livid.

"What an atrocious thing to say! At least Jake isn't arrogant enough to pretend he's Mr. Mystery Man."

Raleigh stood quietly, and now his face was cold and closed. Only his light eyes seemed alive, and they examined her with tight fury. When he spoke, his voice was barely audible.

"Clearly, I should have given you a dossier with all my personal information in it before I offered to drive you around. Unfortunately I didn't."

In three strides he was in his car, and Claire was still scowling at him as he yelled from his window: "Eight o'clock tomorrow, Claire."

She cursed at his dust as he pulled away.

Damn the man. He was messing her all up and down, causing her to lose her temper as if she cared. She hadn't done that for years. Nothing on this earth would get her in the car with him tomorrow. She'd walk barefoot for hours rather than kowtow to his insufferable arrogance. Of all the nerve. Yelling to her as if she were a naughty schoolgirl. She would ask Jolly's Juan to give her a lift. She would ask him right now. Impulsively, she slammed closed her trailer door and started up the road, riding on her adrenaline and anger.

She hadn't stomped a few steps before her mood simmered down to controlled seriousness. She was overwrought. The pressures of finishing up her project were stretching her thinner than she had realized. With a sense of loss, it occurred to her she had forgotten Raleigh's photography book in his car; the whole trip to the hotel had been useless. It counteracted her anger, mixing her emotions.

After a few more paces, she put her fists in her pockets, turned around and walked back to her trailer. It would be good to see Jolly, but she could wash her face and have a bit to eat first. She smiled ruefully at herself, picturing Jolly's expression if she were to descend upon her in her present state. Jolly would throw up her hands and laugh at her.

# Take 4 Books an Umbrella & Mystery Gift— FREE

**And preview exciting new Silhouette Romance novels every month—as soon as they're published!**

# Silhouette Romance®

# Yes...Get 4 Silhouette Romance novels (a $7.80 value) a Folding Umbrella & Mystery Gift FREE!

**Debbie Macomber's CHRISTMAS MASQUERADE.** Jo Marie met Andrew, her dream man, in the crush of a Mardi Gras parade. By Christmas, he was another woman's fiancé. Why, Jo Marie wondered, didn't he seem happy with his intended? And why was Jo Marie back in his arms tonight? Could Andrew still be her dream man?

**Emilie Richards' GILDING THE LILY.** Lesley Belmont had always held back—from success, from men, from love. Now, she had a chance to interview Travis Hagen, America's premier cartoonist. One look, and one kiss from the dynamic Travis and Lesley knew her days of holding back were gone forever.

**Rita Rainville's WRITTEN ON THE WIND.** Handwriting analyst Dena Trevor has to convince acting company president Brand McAllister that her expertise can expose a company spy. Level-headed Brand has to convince himself that he is not falling in love with the beautiful Dena.

**Arlene James' NOW OR NEVER.** Mary Judith could sense that new handyman Nolan Tanner was hiding a secret. She also knew just one touch from Nolan could unlock the secret of her own pent-up emotions. Living under the same boardinghouse roof made their love seem so right...if only Mary Judith could discover Nolan's secret.

**SLIP AWAY FOR AWHILE...** Let Silhouette Romance draw you into a world of fascinating men and women. You'll find it's easy to close the door on the cares and concerns of everyday life as you lose yourself in the timeless drama of love, played out in exotic locations the world over.

**EVERY BOOK AN ORIGINAL...** Every Silhouette Romance is a full-length story, never before in print, superbly written by your favorite authors to give you more of what you want from romance. Start with these 4 Silhouette Romance novels—a $7.80 value—FREE with the attached coupon. Along with your Folding Umbrella and Mystery Gift, they are a present from us to you, with no obligation to buy anything now or ever.

**NO OBLIGATION...** Each month we'll send you 6 brand-new Silhouette Romance novels. Your books will be sent to you as soon as they are published, without obligation. If not enchanted, simply return them within 15 days and owe nothing. Or keep them, and pay just $11.70. And there's never any additional charge for shipping and handling.

**SPECIAL EXTRAS FOR HOME SUBSCRIBERS ONLY...** When you take advantage of this offer and become a home subscriber, we'll also send you the Silhouette Books Newsletter FREE with each book shipment. Every informative issue features news about upcoming titles, interviews with your favorite authors, even their favorite recipes.

So send in the postage-paid card today, and take your fantasies further than they've ever been. The trip will do you good!

CLIP AND MAIL THIS POSTPAID CARD TODAY!

NO POSTAGE
NECESSARY
IF MAILED
IN THE
UNITED STATES

**BUSINESS REPLY MAIL**
FIRST CLASS. PERMIT NO. 194 CLIFTON, N.J.

*Postage will be paid by addressee*

**Silhouette Books**
**120 Brighton Road**
**P.O. Box 5084**
**Clifton, NJ 07015-9956**

**Take your fantasies further than they've ever been. Get 4 Silhouette Romance novels (a $7.80 value) plus a Folding Umbrella & Mystery Gift FREE!**

Then preview future novels for 15 days—
FREE and without obligation. Details inside.

**Your happy endings begin right here.**

# Silhouette Romance ®

**Silhouette Books, 120 Brighton Rd., P.O. Box 5084, Clifton, NJ 07015-9956**

☐ YES! Please send me my four Silhouette Romance novels along with my FREE Folding Umbrella and Mystery Gift, as explained in this insert. I understand that I am under no obligation to purchase any books.

NAME _____
(please print)

ADDRESS _____

CITY _____ STATE _____ ZIP _____

Terms and prices subject to change.
Your enrollment is subject to acceptance by Silhouette Books.

CTR076

"Claire, nothing is important enough to give you such flurry," she would say, and she would be right.

Damn the man.

The clean-face prospect turned into a quick shower, and with an apple to take the edge off her hunger, Claire started once more for Jolly's. The dust next to the road kicked up into her shoes, a dry grit that suited her exactly. After the tensions and stimulations of the day, walking down a late-afternoon road was the perfect thing to do, but even so, part of her couldn't relax. From a distance, she saw that Jolly's Date Stand was empty. The umbrella had been taken down and only the card table stood in the usually busy spot. People were picking up last-minute items for dinner, and even as Claire watched, a car slowed down to take a look. As it drove away, she hurried on, wondering what could have happened, and thinking of the children.

Everything was still. Then she spied Jolly seated in a folding chair in the shady grove of date palms. The matron was holding a steaming cup in her two hands and tapping one of her little feet in an uneven rhythm, timing a tune inaudible to anyone but herself. She looked up as Claire approached, and the foot stopped.

"Hello, Jolly. Isn't it early for the date stand to be closed?"

She shrugged.

"I got tired of it."

The foot resumed its tapping, and Claire began to feel uncomfortable. Something wasn't right. The date stand closed for an afternoon was unusual, but Jolly being less than friendly was simply unheard of. Jolly wasn't even looking at her. Claire took a step nearer and sat on the stunted grass next to the chair, leaning her head back in an effort to ease her neck. She shut her eyes, letting the rustle of the palms and the bird noises sift into her consciousness. Then she reached out the only way she could.

"I don't know what's wrong, Jolly, but I don't think I'll be able to stand it if on top of everything, you won't talk to me."

Jolly took a shrewd glance at her and immediately became warmly businesslike.

"You poor honey. All tired out and me being a grump. You just sit there and I'll get you a hot cup of something. I don't suppose you want a little of my own, no. Some tea maybe." Without waiting for an answer, she got up and trod lightly into her house, emerging a minute later with another folding chair and then a cup of hot water with a teabag. She didn't sit down again until Claire was in the new chair and had taken a sip.

"It's not really Salada," she confessed, as Claire picked up the tag. "I just like the fortunes so my daughter-in-law sends them to me and I put them on the saucer whenever I have a cup. It's kind of nice that way. I've gotten to know them all and I can pick my fortune. What's yours say?"

Claire smiled. Who but Jolly? She flipped the little red hexagon, holding it in a patch of sunlight.

"'Nothing succeeds like apple pie.' Jolly! How on earth? What does this have to do with anything?" She couldn't believe it.

Jolly chuckled infectiously.

"I thought you'd get a kick out of it." Her eyes crinkled to slits as she laughed, and she shook all over until she had to slow down and wipe away a tear. "Heavens! I suppose that's what I get for being serious all afternoon. When I finally get laughing again I might as well explode." She subsided into a good grin, and then she gestured toward Claire's Ace bandage.

"I'd heard you hurt the wrist. How's it doing?"

"How did you know?"

"Frank up at the hotel told me. Then he winked. I knew there wasn't something stuck in his eye so I just asked him what that wink was for. He hedged around a bit—Frank's like that—but I finally got it out of him. Since I'd already seen you drive by this morning, I knew the wind had something in it. Now I want to hear all about it."

Clair felt the color creeping into her face and silently cursed her fair complexion for the millionth time. She had expected Jolly to be nosy, and she shouldn't have been surprised by the lack of subtlety, but such blunt tactics were enough to knock her over. She admired the unknown Frank's ability to hedge for even a little while. She took a gulp of tea and scalded the roof of her mouth.

"Don't you get tongue-tied on me now, girl. I want the whole story, right from hello-and-pleased-to-meet-you."

Claire hitched one of her feet up onto the chair and settled in. Then she began with the night on the road when Raleigh had had a flat. After a couple of stops and starts, the rest of it all came rushing out, right up to the tiff they had just had. Jolly pulled absently at a bobby pin over her ear as she listened, and Claire was drawn to reveal even more than she realized. She hadn't confided to anyone about anything for so long, and it was a relief just to hear herself talk. She suspected her tangle of emotions was beginning to indicate something, and saw the same suspicions mirrored on Jolly's face. Their cups grew cold. Jolly set hers on the ground and wiped her palms slowly on her skirt before speaking.

"Looks to me like you're experiencing confusion, as we say. I've been concerned about you, Claire. Thought about it this afternoon. Things can happen suddenly out here in the desert; I've seen it. Everything moves all the faster because you don't expect it to. The weather, the sun, the kids. The land here hides things—trouble and happiness, thieves and gold. I've seen it. I've gotten fond of you, and I hope you won't take me wrong, but you better watch yourself. Think now: how much do you know about this man from the hotel?"

Claire shifted in the folding chair and inadvertently swallowed the last cold sip of her tea. What did she know about him? A photographer visiting Sophie Blake. She knew he had atrocious manners in a pinch. He had a wicked sense of humor. He was oddly reticent at times, and proud, and sensitive. He learned quickly. He seemed to be developing some respect for her. He was devastatingly attractive. It was precious little, when she thought about it, but there was something else, too. Something that went beyond the gaps in her knowledge. Some corner of her had linked up with a corner of him ever since that first disturbing encounter. Even in such a short time. She was still terrified to look at it any more closely. What if...? She couldn't begin to explain it to Jolly, but as she turned and looked into that wise face, she realized she didn't need to try.

"I thought so," Jolly said softly, shaking her head. "So angry, so happy. It's like you woke up, yes? You have to live every feeling to the hilt. It doesn't matter how much you don't know about him, I suppose. I just hope you'll keep your eyes open."

She leaned toward Claire and looked her straight in the eye.

"I tell you, that man is not just somebody passing through Death Valley for vacations." She paused, obviously weighing her words. "What do you know about the drug traffic here? I don't mean marijuana and peyote. I mean the trouble stuff. Dust. Heroin."

She was startled.

"Only what Mr. Ecks told me. They bring it up from Mexico, right?"

Jolly nodded, watching her closely, and Claire wondered what she knew. Why did she ask?

"You manage to have your nose in the dust and your head in the clouds at the same time, honey. The whole world could be talking suspicion and trouble all around you and you wouldn't hear. You just watch yourself, and if you need us, we'll stand by you, Juan and me. That's a promise."

Claire shivered in the coolness. Evening had fallen without her noticing, and now the palms were sending eerie shadows around the grove. The birds had hushed and the musty smell of old dates filled the dim air. Jolly had pulled a shawl up around her shoulders, and her stout form merged with the silhouette of a tree trunk behind her. For an instant, she looked different, almost mystical, huddled there in the vague folds of the shawl. Claire shook her head. She was getting fanciful. Yet the warning lingered ominously between them. She laughed, but the sound fell coldly on her ears, and Jolly didn't smile.

"Come on, Jolly, I'm not going to get in trouble." Her voice sounded dry and too loud in the stillness. "I'm far too sensible, and besides, I'm only going to be here for a few more days. I couldn't get mixed up in anything by then, even if I tried."

The door of the house slammed, making them both start, and then Juan Avalos came up behind his wife. He set his hands on her shoulders and smiled at Claire.

"You two have probably settled politics, babies and the hereafter by now. Care to come in for something to eat?"

Jolly reached up and rested a hand on top of his.

"That's a joke, Claire. Juan couldn't scramble an egg if his life depended on it."

"Not true, not true," he said, a bit too offended. "I scrambled an egg just the other day. I admit I didn't cook it afterward, but I did scramble like a pro." He gave Jolly's shoulders a squeeze, and that person groaned as she stood up, mumbling something about pros.

Claire stood too, and handed over her empty cup. "Thanks a lot for the tea, Jolly, and I can't tell you how good it was to sit down for a proper chat. I think you must be wrong about Raleigh, but I'll be careful."

Juan looked at her.

"Raleigh. Is that the guy from the hotel with the green Fiat? He's a friend of yours? Well, that explains it. He goes through as much gas as you do. I'm beginning to think you geologists pick sites all over the place just for the fun of driving there."

"But—"

"That's right," Jolly interrupted. "And Claire's getting a ride along with him now that her wrist is bad."

Juan's smile showed concern.

"I'd heard about that. You got to watch your step around here, that's for sure. If you need any ice, I can get you some."

She assured him that it was doing fine, and declining an invitation for dinner, she headed home.

Her mind was buzzing and she didn't know which idea to start working on first. Heroin! Why on earth had Jolly brought that up? Why had she let Juan believe Raleigh was with Claire? The implication that Raleigh might be in any way mixed up with the drug business was insane. He was just a visiting photographer. That was clear enough. She must be mistaken. And yet, Jolly had a way of knowing things. No. She had to be mistaken. Claire almost ran the short way back to the trailer, locking the door securely behind her and turning on all the lights. The thoughts raced in upon her and she sat down, dazed. It was all very well to be having confusion about a taciturn photographer, but quite another thing to be running around with a potentially dangerous criminal, much less... No. Her mind closed on the thought. She would have to find out more about him because she couldn't bear the suspicions that were crowding around her heart.

Her knapsack was under the table where she had left it and she drew it to her, opening it as if it held the answers inside. The zipper caught and she pulled at it fretfully, then threw the whole bundle back to the floor.

What was she going to do? How could she find out why he was here? The questions nagged at her until another inner demon reared its ugly head.

"Why is it so important to you to know?" it demanded.

"No," she said aloud, wrapping her arms around her. It couldn't be that she cared so much for him. She was just curious and concerned. But images of their day together came back to haunt her. Their moment at Dante's View, his laughing eyes, his throwing the rock up the canyon, and finally the way he had touched her cheek, standing so close. If only he had told her then what he was thinking.

With a quirk of suspicion, she realized his "appointment" might have been the meeting with Sophie on the terrace. But he could have told her that. What a foursome they had made. She recalled her own unusual behavior with excruciating embarrassment. How Sophie had gloated! She was mortified. Raleigh had become so distant and critical, and then... Oh, why had she exploded at him? Now that her anger was gone, she was seized by a lurking dread. Would they be able to straighten it out tomorrow? Whatever else he might be, he couldn't be a criminal.

Heroin. It was absurd. She laughed aloud, but with short-lived humor. She got up and paced the short distance to her darkroom and back. So she was feeling more than fond of him. Okay. She could handle that. She was not one of those people who became useless and miserable the first chance they got to care for someone. She refused to be vulnerable. She would stand on her own, and clear up this ridiculous idea that he might have anything to do with heroin. A little strength. Some spine. She would meet him tomorrow and either find out why he was here, or put off the rest of her work until Harris could come and help.

Harris! There was another problem. When did he say he was coming? The sixteenth, day after tomorrow. Well, she thought, that would work out all right; she could wait a day. Suddenly she sat down again, stunned. She had forgotten all about the fifteenth.

Tomorrow was the Ides of March, and Claire's twenty-fourth birthday.

## Chapter Seven

The fifteenth was already several hours old, and a mass of gray clouds threatened to settle in and smother anything living in Death Valley. Claire sat in the passenger seat of Raleigh's car and felt her stomach sinking. The static in the weather had affected her nervous system, adding anxiety to the tension that already hunched in her shoulders. Her courage of the evening before had left her the minute Raleigh had knocked on her trailer door, and now the silence sat old between them like a tangible thing. Unable to broach the subject that gnawed at her, she dismissed every other topic as too trite to mention. What could she talk about? Last night's tiff? Right. The weather? Absurd. Why was he frowning? That least of all. The distance hurried beneath them, their wheels pushing it along. Claire tried in vain to shake off her uneasiness.

Raleigh shifted gears and slowed the Fiat until the engine was rumbling in an idle. Then he pulled off the road. Claire looked ahead and behind, but the road stretched empty in both directions. They weren't anywhere near Salt Creek yet. She was dumbfounded. What on earth was he doing now? He rested an arm on the steering wheel and turned to face her. With a prickle of anticipation, she avoided his eyes and focused instead on his ear.

"There you go again. Quit making that face at me," he said. "I don't know how long you can keep up this suffering silence bit, but I sure don't intend to find out."

A lump clutched at her throat. What was he doing? She felt as uncomfortable as a petulant child, wanting to declare innocence, but knowing she was more inclined to pout. The one thing she knew for sure was that she resented his tone of voice.

"Of all the nerve," she spat out. "Maybe I don't feel like chatting. Did you think of that? Maybe I don't feel like talking to you at all. Maybe . . . you might try being a little more pleasant instead of sitting there like a . . . like a lump."

To her complete dismay, tears welled up behind her lids and she had to close her eyes to hold them back. What was wrong with her?

"Hey," he said, and then went on more softly. "I didn't realize—hey, cut that out. You're making me nervous."

Claire issued a watery chuckle and got a grip on herself. It was just like him to be thinking of himself when a strange woman was crying in his car. He was watching her with a quiet concern that belied his teasing, and when she finally met his blue gaze, the connection was so direct she could feel comfort coming from him as surely as if he had put his arm around her. This couldn't be real. She dug a tissue out of her pocket and blew her nose.

"This doesn't happen very often, I assure you," she began.

"Don't be stupid. Something's really bothering you, and I won't flatter myself thinking me being a lump, as you put it, has anything to do with it."

He ran a hand along the wheel, and looked at her, waiting. It was clearly an invitation to tell him what was bothering her, but he couldn't know that he himself was the cause of her turmoil. If only it were something else, some problem with her geology or her photography. A sickness in the family. But it wasn't. Raleigh watched the emotions run across her flushed face, and misread her hesitance for distrust. He closed his grip around the wheel and looked away from her. Immediately she felt the loss of a chance wasted. The lofty exterior crept up, blocking her out before she fully realized it had been down, and she knew his effort to help her had been a rare thing for him.

"Of course, you don't need to confide in me," he said dryly.

It was too late. It seemed they never connected properly, and she succumbed to the idea they never would. He pulled the Fiat back onto the road. Her reserves of strength and self-confidence were sapped, or she would have tried to set things straight between them right then. In a daze, she stared dismally out the window. What a day this was turning out to be.

"It's my birthday," she whispered, without thinking. She was watching the road, but she felt his eyes flick briefly to her. They drove for a while, and she heard a noise in his throat. Now what? She looked over at his profile. He was smiling! Of all the—! Slowly, the humor of it hit her, too. You would think she had just lost twenty years of her life, the way she was carrying on.

"How old are you?" he asked, his voice dead even.

Claire tipped her chin up at him and suppressed a sudden laugh.

"Guess?"

He grinned, and then thought for a second.

"Well, when I watch your face, I could swear you just turned seventeen. You have too much enthusiasm. You're too gullible." A grin took out the sting. "Then I listen to your voice, and you sound so serious. It takes wisdom and hard knocks to say the things you do sometimes. It could just be because your voice is low. I don't know. You might be twenty-eight, twenty-nine."

Claire was pleased. He had an odd way of giving a compliment, and she wasn't immune.

"I don't think you're giving us much credit. I was much more serious at seventeen than I could ever be when I'll be twenty-eight. Besides, I'm only one age at a time. You come up with a pretty broad spread for an educated guess."

Raleigh flipped on the windshield wipers as the first light drops of rain fell.

"I don't think I've given you permission to refer to my education, broad or otherwise," he commented wryly. "Besides, you're the one who told me to guess. You couldn't guess my age."

"Thirty-three," she said, without hesitation.

"Who did you ask?"

Claire smiled.

"Nobody. Maybe you just remind me of someone I know who is thirty-three." An image of her brother surfaced in her memory.

"And who would that be?"

"I don't believe I've given you permission to refer to my education," she echoed smoothly.

He chuckled.

"I guess that means we're even."

They pulled into a small parking lot where signs and a boardwalk led to Salt Creek. She reached back to get her sack. It was light enough for her to handle one-handedly today, and she motioned Raleigh not to bother getting out.

"You don't need to get wet too," she said.

He nodded.

"I'll just head back to the hotel. When will you be done?"

Claire checked her watch and waited for a roll of thunder to stop before answering.

"Around 11:30."

"I'll be here at 11:30 then, and then you'll have to keep your half of the deal. We have some sightseeing to do."

"In this?" she asked, getting out of the car and holding up a hand in the traditional rain-catching pose.

Raleigh just grinned, and reached over to pull the door closed. She heard him honk as she started up the boardwalk and, as the sound echoed away, she realized she was suddenly very alone, in the rain, in the middle of nowhere.

Claire stood and arched her back, slowing looking across the salt flats. The rain had lasted only a few minutes, drenching everything and exhausting the clouds. Now the flatness was covered by shimmery, throbbing air, as the sun burned off the moisture.

She leaned over, collecting her pencils and notebook. She awkwardly put them inside her sack, probably for the last time. Her left hand was better, but still not good enough to use for any period of time. Thank goodness she had nearly finished her project before that eventful fall in Ubehebe. There was no way she could complete the extra work she had wanted to, but with Raleigh's help, at least she had done all she had outlined in her proposal. She smiled at the sluggish pool on her left. The very last site on her list. It was incredible to be finished. She almost sat back in the mud as the thought sank in. This was the end of her research! It was only a matter of pulling it all together, and then she would actually be leaving.

Leaving. Perhaps as soon as Harris came. The thought dulled her excitement, and she paused to absorb her mix of emotions. She would miss the desert, and working outside at all hours of the day. She would miss her funny little trailer. It wouldn't matter anymore that she couldn't drive the Scout. She would no longer have any reason to impose on Raleigh's generosity. She felt a stirring in her stomach. Even more than that, she would be leaving, and she'd probably never see him again. She didn't like the idea at all.

She had been frightened when he had left her alone in the rain, wishing she had told someone else where she was in case anything were to happen to him and he couldn't come back. There had been nothing to do, however, and she had started up the boardwalk that led next to the creek and down a shallow dip in the land. She would have enjoyed having him along, like when they were in Titus Canyon. A professor had told her about Salt Creek a few years before, and as the rain smacked against the creek and the trails of water ran past her feet in little streams, a flood of thoughts came back. Besides being left wet in a strange place, she had no one to share

her thoughts with. It didn't occur to her that she had
been on her own in similar situations for months now,
and it hadn't bothered her.

The scarcity of water in the desert naturally made it
the focus of the history, and Salt Creek had its stories
like any other place. An early team of covered wagons
had stopped there, and for lack of wood the travelers
had had to burn a wagon to smoke their oxen meat. It
left a lot unsaid, that story did. Raleigh would have
thought so too. She had walked from Salt Creek to
McClean Spring when the rain was slowing to a drizzle
and the smells were seeping out of the sun-baked earth.

Now her clothes had dried and her notes were put
away for good. Finished! She couldn't get over it. She
longed to be able to absorb the stark beauty of the vista
before her, but between her excitement and her anxiousness, her mind was too easily distracted. For the first
time, the serenity was lost on her. She sighed, giving up,
and allowed her thoughts to go back to Raleigh. They
seemed to belong there. His name rang through her
head, putting a smile onto her face as she thought of
spending the afternoon with him. She must make the
most of it, since it might be their last.

As if they had had many. This is getting ridiculous,
she said to herself. You are not an inexperienced
schoolgirl who's never seen anything in pants. This is
nothing to get excited about. Sure, there seemed to be an
extraordinary attraction between them, but it was frus-
trating as often as intriguing. There was no point re-
hearsing her memories to death. For instance, why
consider that surprise afternoon in Shoshone? Why remember his tall form as she'd first seen it beside the
garage? Something clicked.

She had forgotten about the stranger. What had Raleigh been doing there anyway? She never had learned. In fact, he never explained why— No. She was not going to begin this again. She tried to ignore the thoughts but the turmoil began again, until she stood up with impatience. She couldn't even dictate her own state of mind about the man.

She lifted her sack and took a final look at McClean Spring before she headed back toward the boardwalk at Salt Creek. She had come a good mile and a half across the salt, and now, without the cloud cover, the ground glared with a white heat. She had forgotten her sunglasses because of the rain, so it took a good squint to see up the rough path.

From the corner of her eye, she saw something flash on the far cliff, and she raised a hand against the sun to get a better look. For a long minute she studied the steep wall, and then she saw the flash again. Someone was up there with field glasses; that was the only explanation. She looked around to see what the person could be watching, but the brief rain had washed out any tracks or patterns the viewer could have seen from his perch, and no birds ventured across the sky. The only thing in view would be herself. Claire felt the skin crawl on the back of her neck and hurried back to the boardwalk. The ghosts of the early travelers were playing tricks on her eyes. She walked rapidly, hoping Raleigh would be on time.

When she reached the boardwalk, she checked back, but could no longer see the place where the flash had come from. Still, the newly washed silence of the creek did nothing to dispel the eeriness, and she couldn't wait to see the last of the shallow gulch. The walk took her longer than she expected; the hot air clung to her as she moved, slowing her pace the more she hurried. A nervous glance at her watch told her it was a quarter to twelve. She was still several hundred yards away from the parking lot when she saw Raleigh coming quickly toward her up the boardwalk, his long strides heavy on the new wood. Claire's heart raced, and her whole body relaxed in relief.

"There you are," he observed. "I was just beginning to think I shouldn't have left you out here all alone. Did you get into some kind of trouble?"

"You underestimate me," she said, still shaken, and thinking how closely he had read her mind. With his reassuring solidness before her, she smiled, and wondered what it could have been that had made her so nervous a few minutes before. He was watching her, and suddenly she felt shy. He had been on time, and concerned, and her worry had been for nothing. The sun felt good on her cheek, and she dearly would have liked to sling her arm through his.

"You look smug. What have you been doing?" He looked around, as if the earth itself would give him the answer.

Claire told him briefly about McClean Spring and the notes she had taken there. He listened with one ear as they walked down the boardwalk, and then he stopped her.

"Do geologists know anything about bugs? See those things swimming in there? They've been upside down like that the whole way. What are they?"

Claire laughed, looking where he pointed, and began to explain about the insect life. Her professor had done her research on the caddis-fly population here, and Claire was able to tell him about the different creatures that could tolerate the salty water. It was wonderful to think that the fish and insects in this area were descendants from a time when all of Death Valley had been covered by the huge, still, Lake Manly. Raleigh listened attentively. The lake had vanished, leaving sands and sediment behind. This led her to her favorite topic, of course, and as they got into the car, she rambled happily on, telling the history of the valley. Her own research had made it a fairy tale to her, a story of change and patience that went far beyond any study she could have read in a book. Her eyes sparkled as she talked, until she realized he hadn't gotten a word in edgewise.

"What got me going like that? You must be bored out of your wits. Why didn't you stop me?" she finally asked, amazed at herself, and not a little embarrassed. She was so unused to talking for long stretches that she didn't realize she could easily sustain someone's interest. There was nothing she dreaded so much as a bore.

"You underestimate me," he replied.

Claire chuckled.

"I suppose I deserve that."

Raleigh shifted his grip on the steering wheel.

"No, I mean it. This valley has puzzled me, and I've wanted to know more about it, now that I've been here a while. I just never wanted to ask Mr. Ecks, and Sophie didn't have any literature about it. I suppose I'm just lazy."

She was inwardly pleased that he admitted he was interested, but bit her lip at the reference to Sophie. She had been forgetting her. Was this his way of reminding her? Yesterday had been more than effective in reasserting Sophie's status. But then, Raleigh was an unusual guest to be roaming off all the time the way he did. What did Sophie think of it, or did their relationship put no limits on the daylight hours? It was a catty thought, and

Claire was immediately contrite, even though she had said nothing aloud. She fiddled with the doorknob.

"How is Sophie?"

He glanced over at her, amused.

"I wondered when you would ask about her. She asks about you often enough, and last night would have been the grand Inquisition itself if I hadn't been in such a bad mood that she was scared off. This morning she was pouting because the rain interfered with her golf plans. She had to reschedule seven people to a bridge table, and she was not very excited about it. The last I saw of her she was trying to get hold of Jake, but quite frankly, I doubt it would do her any good. I think our astronomer is wise to her, and besides, I don't believe he plays."

Claire didn't know what to make of his tone. It held a sardonic edge, almost mocking, but that couldn't be the case if he were a dear friend of Sophie's.

"Why didn't you stay to be the eighth?" she asked, honestly curious.

His profile looked stern, but his tone was, if possible, even lighter.

"What? And leave you to celebrate your birthday alone?"

"Oh, that," she said, glad to have a different topic. "I wouldn't have been alone. I think I'll take Jolly up on her perpetual invitation to dinner. Say, where are you taking me anyway?"

He grinned again.

"Your curiosity is getting slower. Where do you guess?"

She was getting accustomed to his challenging way of baiting her, and her own wits raced as she tried to surpass his. She started naming improbable, obscure places, and waited for his reaction. He wouldn't tell their true destination until she could have wrung his neck with great satisfaction, and finally they passed a sign.

"Of course. I should have guessed. A sham like you would naturally want to see the home of the biggest humbug Death Valley has ever known."

She was kidding, but he hesitated before laughing. Did he always? She stored away the pause to be thought about more carefully later, adding it to the pile. Did Scotty's Castle have something to do with his presence here? Watch yourself, a voice reminded her, but she was enjoying herself too much. Today was her birthday. She could be careful tomorrow.

They arrived just as a tour was beginning, and hurried to buy their tickets at a miniature gazebo in the yard. Scotty's Castle was a wonder in adobe and carved wood. With her first step through the gate and into the cool courtyard, Claire knew she was going to enjoy herself thoroughly. She smiled at Raleigh, unaware of what an entrancing picture she presented, with her eyes all earnest like a child's. She looked from side to side, peeking curiously at the tiles and shadows. Pretty sights beckoned her from every corner. A century before, a desert cottage had been built for Mrs. Johnson by her millionaire husband Albert. The little palace indulged in all the whimsy and extravagance that Death Valley Scotty had been able to inspire in his two friends, and Scotty had been a persuasive, endearing hoodlum. Plans for the swimming pool were never completed, but fountains, tiled terraces and balconies abounded. Their guide led them from one huge comfortable room to the next, pointing out the obvious as well as the subtle, for even the dullest tourist. He regaled them with the folklore that had sprung up with it, dwelling upon hidden doors and decadence. It was an absurd, fanciful place, ridiculously situated in the middle of nowhere, but there was clearly a genius behind it all. The little group was enthralled. When Claire whispered to Raleigh her delight in one of the beautiful stained-glass lamps, the guide interrupted his commentary long enough to warn him: "Watch out, or she'll be wanting one for your living room."

Claire was startled and mildly perplexed, but Raleigh merely chuckled and smugly folded his arms. When the implication sank in, she blushed and turned shocked eyes to Raleigh. He was letting them think they were a couple! He saw her confusion and grinned all the more, daring her to undeceive them. An elderly woman in the group smiled at them both and traded glances with her husband. By the end of the tour, much against Claire's wishes, she and her grinning escort were established as the token young couple, and served as the brunt of any number of good-natured jokes. As they walked out the big gate, the elderly woman leaned over and patted Claire's arm.

"Don't you let him push you around, dear," she said, and winked.

Claire stuttered out something and threw a reproachful look at Raleigh. He laughed aloud, and put a possessive arm around her waist. She stiffened, untrusting of his playfulness.

"We really can't disappoint them, can we," he whispered, and leaning close, he kissed her. It was intended as a harmless gesture, but it was a final straw.

Claire raised her hand to slap him, and quicker than instinct, he caught her wrist in a steely grip. His face hardened and then he kissed her again, this time deliberately, holding her until he was finished. She wrenched free and stepped back, gasping. Never had she been treated like this. She winced in a delayed reaction to being restrained, and biting words sprang to her tongue. The wary smile on Raleigh's face reminded her they were not alone, and with supreme effort she controlled her fury.

"You wretch," she hissed. "You only do that to me in public, don't you, so I can't hit you like you deserve."

Watching his despicable smile freeze, she took another step back and nearly fell into a low ditch behind her. He reached forward quickly to catch her, but she shook off his hand and regained her balance. She eyed the ditch and then him, as if he were responsible for putting it there.

"You should watch your step," he said, with meaning.

Fire glinted in her eyes as the air between them bristled, and his cool veneer barely hid a stronger emotion. The other tourists had wandered away, leaving them alone, and she felt strangely vulnerable. Suddenly her knees felt soft, and she began to shake. What had happened here? His kiss had thrown her composure in whirls, and her bruised lips burned. The thought of getting into the car for the ride back with him gave her heart a jerk.

"I want to buy a postcard," she said lamely, grasping for any kind of delay. "I'll meet you in a minute."

Without waiting for his nod, she turned and made her way across the yard to the little shop. The sun was hot on her bare arms, and the bright reflections off the adobe made her dizzy. Reaching for the porch post, she stepped into the shade and took several long, slow breaths. She was shaken, no doubt about it. Did he have this kind of effect upon everyone? She blushed again and put a hand up to her cheek. This would not do. Gripping the post and running a hand through her hair, she looked out on the yard, trying to concentrate on what she saw there. People were coming and going as usual, unaware of the pale, wide-eyed woman on the porch. She watched a man roll a wheelbarrow around a stump and brace it against his hip while he shook out his hand. Above him, the pines climbed on the hillside, nearly washed clear of color by the full sunlight. The scene didn't even bother to mock her; it simply didn't care one jot for her insignificant problems.

It wasn't the first time since knowing him that she wished she'd had more experience with men of Raleigh's cut. Her inconsistency surprised even herself, but she knew it wasn't due to lack of intelligence or self-confidence. She simply hadn't put in the hours. She didn't know what to do with him.

She reached into her pocket and pulled out her change purse, opening it awkwardly with the bad hand. Then she stepped into the store and selected a couple of postcards. The clerk's indifferent smile settled the last of her agitation, and she slipped the postcards under her elbow. She would send one to her old roommate in Manhattan; she collected postcards. She'd send the other to her uncle. How he would tease if he knew she'd been so disturbed by a kiss. He'd say her innocence was showing. She smiled wistfully, remembering the joke. She would have to give him a call later. Pausing to straighten her hair and retuck her white blouse, she headed out to look for Raleigh.

He wasn't where she had left him, and she stood for a moment looking around. Curious, she thought she heard his voice, and followed it to a temporary workman's

shed near the treacherous ditch. Sure enough, it was
Raleigh, and he was talking to a young, gawky boy. The
boy kept glancing furtively over his shoulder, and
touching one ear as if with a nervous tic. His eyes had a
weary, haunted look she had seen in newspaper photos.
Quickly, she spun around and walked back to the store.
What were they doing? Had Raleigh gotten rid of her
intentionally, in order to speak to that boy? No, she had
suggested herself that she buy a postcard. He couldn't
have anticipated that. It might be a harmless, coinci-
dental meeting. But then what were they doing in the
shed? She stood stupidly on the porch, trying to figure
it out. Unbidden, Jolly's warnings surfaced in her mind,
and an icy blanket numbed her nerves. It didn't matter
how it happened; Raleigh could have managed to have
a clandestine moment without her any number of ways,
no matter what she'd done. Her eyes were looking, unseeing, at the phone booth, and automatically, she
stepped toward it. She needed to call someone. This was
just too unreal.

On instinct, she lifted the receiver and put through a
collect call to her uncle's home in Chicago. As the bell
rang at the other end, she hoped it was late enough there
for him to be back from his office, and an instant later,
his voice was asking her hello.

"It's me, Uncle Chaz."

"Claire? Happy birthday, old girl! We were just hoping you would call. How are you doing?"

It was so fine to hear his big, warm voice. The relief
flooded through her worries like rain down a dusty
drainpipe. She could almost smell his tobacco right there
in the phone booth, and it made her long to be home.

Explaining that she only had a minute, she sketched
her progress with her project and said she'd be back in

Chicago in a matter of days. Then, with a twinge of butterflies, she added: "You wouldn't happen to know anything about narcotics traffic, would you? I know this sounds dumb, but do you know anything about the kind of people who do the setups?"

There was a pause, and she could imagine the big man choosing his words. His voice came serious and guarded.

"Just a little. You know how things are here. I can tell you you shouldn't be involved in anything, no matter how clear-cut and simple it looks. These people are ingenious. The good ones look like your next-door neighbor; you'd never know. If you're in trouble, I'll be there on the next plane. I can—"

"No, no, no," she said. "I'm not in trouble." At least, she thought, not the kind of trouble an uncle could help with. "I was just wondering. Look, I have to go, but I'll call again soon. Love to Betty and Jeremy."

She hung up. Raleigh had come across the yard and spied her just as she stepped out of the booth. From his expression, he had not expected to find her making a call, but as he reached her he merely waited. Claire was pale, but she managed a smile and askcd if he was ready to go. His eyebrows lifted slightly in continued surprise, and he nodded.

"You got your cards?"

She had forgotten all about them, but there they were under her elbow. That settled everything. Thc two of them walked silently to the car, Claire keeping pace with him but edgy as a cat. She avoided his eyes as he opened the door for her, and when she accidentally brushed his arm as she got in, she almost jumped. As they pulled out on the road again, he gave her a sideways glance.

"We are not going to do another silence-and-quarrel routine. If you want an apology, I'll give it to you right now. I didn't know you were so touchy. In any case, I shouldn't have done that, but when you look at me in just that way, it's like a kitten saying 'I dare ya,' and God knows I never could pass up a dare."

Claire didn't know what to say. A kitten was the last thing she felt like, except for the claws and the nerves. Then again, at least it was an apology, even if it was a cocky one. He didn't explain anything either. She was tiring of this sidestepping, as if neither one of them knew something was going on. Why didn't she just ask him point-blank who that man had been?

"I'll give you this: you sure can hold a grudge."

His voice was so mournful she had to laugh, and once she had, she couldn't regain her scolding demeanor. The devil.

"I tell you what," she said. "You don't kiss me in public again, and I won't hold it against you."

"Touché. I see now I should have let you hit me. I'll take your deal, though, and just to make it official, why don't you let me take you out to dinner? For your birthday."

She was surprised. That smile of his could probably charm a goldfish out of its bowl. One minute she was resolving to get away from him as soon as possible, the next she was repressing a giddy thrill at the prospect of dinner.

"That would be nice," she said calmly. "I don't know about any of the restaurants out here though. If you like to cook, I suppose we could make dinner in my trailer. You'd have to promise to be on your best behavior, of course."

He smiled at the road and made his voice very serious.

"I think that could be arranged. And in fact, I'm so tired of the restaurants here, a normal meal would be a relief."

They discussed different menus on the way back, and finally Raleigh said he'd manage it all by himself. He insisted, despite her doubts, and she agreed he could get the groceries while she tamed the mess in her trailer. He dropped her off at the trailer and they set an hour. Claire sat on her stoop in the afternoon shade and asked herself whether she was coming or going.

# Chapter Eight

Claire heard the Fiat pull up and opened the trailer door, stepping out into the late sunshine. She was clad in a loose blouse of creamy green, and her sole pair of dress slacks. She had caught some of her hair up over her ear, softening the expanse of her forehead and fully revealing her lovely, luminous eyes. Her slacks made her newly aware of how her figure had been toned from all her exercise, and it was a slightly self-conscious smile she offered to Raleigh. He straightened out of the car, and started across the gravel toward her. His answering smile was frankly appreciative. When he had come about halfway, he stopped and laughed.

"I'll be right there," he said, turning about-face and going back to collect the groceries from the car. Claire watched, feeling singularly pleased with herself, as he balanced two grocery bags and a cassette player, and banged the door closed with his knee. He started toward her again, an appealing jumble of brown and blue, and with a sideways grin that was enough to make her heart miss a beat.

Two hours before, Claire had started cleaning up her trailer and had balked at the enormity of the task. She had been outwitted by her own mess; she simply had too many piles of too many papers, and none of them could be dumped together. Besides that, she had several days' worth of dishes teetering in the sink, and her left hand was practically useless. She was sitting on the couch, trying unsuccessfully to devise a plan, when Jolly Avalos peeked her head through the open door. She carried a bouquet of wildflowers and a card from one of the little ones, while the warm, understanding look in her eyes was the finest birthday present Claire could have wished for.

"Oh, honey. Is it that bad?" Jolly asked.

Instantly Claire realized she'd blown things out of proportion, and with Jolly's help they were soon getting the dishes and the rest under control. Jolly suggested putting the papers in the darkroom laid out in their present disarray. Obviously. Claire was amazed she hadn't thought of it herself, so off they went. The flowers ended up in a tall jar on the little table, and in no time at all, Claire was sitting down again. She was pleased at the difference order and a little colorful life made in the plain room. Trust Jolly to know.

Jolly gave her another concerned smile as she was leaving, and after pursing her lips and trying to hold it back, she'd had to let the advice come out.

"Don't you do something you'd regret, Claire. When I told you to be sleeping in late, I was thinking of something lasting, like. You and that big man, you're not going to be together forever in the desert; but a wicked memory, it can last a long time."

She hurried away on her light feet before Claire could answer her, and in the sudden vacancy of the doorway, she thought her shadow lingered for a second before following. For a salt-of-the-earth person, there was something uncanny about Jolly.

Or maybe it was just the desert itself.

Now Raleigh was filling the same spot the shadow had held, with a solidity that couldn't be doubted. The heavy sun wrapped them in a glow of orange light as they stood facing each other, tacitly enjoying their meeting, and then she stepped aside to let him in. He set the groceries on the couch and looked around, ending at Claire.

"Is this the same place?" he asked in genuine surprise. "What did you do, throw everything out the back window?"

He grinned as he said it, and she shrugged modestly, secretly thinking he had come close to the truth. Even clean, the place was smaller having Raleigh's tall form inside it. He was wearing a deep-blue chamois shirt and a well-cut pair of black trousers. He carried his clothes with that unconscious comfort she had noted before, and now he stood disturbingly close, she had a temptation to smooth the pocket over his heart. She looked up to his face, and found there an expression that almost invited her to do it. Her own heart did a skip. This would not do.

She turned suddenly and started rustling in the bags.

"What did you bring?" she asked.

He chuckled, as if letting her break the tension for the moment, but a resonance remained in the air between them, promising something to come.

"I thought I'd try something wild. You have to sit and do nothing. No interference. This is your birthday and you've got a bum wrist, and for once I don't want any arguments.''

"Okay," she agreed humbly.

He frowned at her, and then they were laughing again. As it turned out, since he didn't know where anything was in the miniature kitchen and she had found ingenious places to hide things, she did quite a bit of interfering. She tried to make it seem like as little as possible. Nobody was fooled, and finally he handed her a spoon.

"You can watch the noodles."

Big of him.

"What are we making?" she asked again.

"Raleigh's Desert Delight."

"No, really."

He grinned.

"Come on, what is it?"

He wouldn't tell.

Just like the turkey, she thought. He doesn't tell anything, just to be exasperating. Devilish, cocky man.

He laughed again, gesturing at her with a tomato.

"I love watching you get annoyed. I've never seen such a transparent face. You must have gotten yourself into a lot of trouble with that complexion of yours."

"I resent that. My face is positively oblique at times, and besides, I don't know what complexion you're talking about." She blinked disarmingly, and he groaned.

Together they cut, cooked and simmered, each bantering and dosing out advice to the other. Every little thing became amusing, from the napkins in the sugar canister to the lack of pepper. Claire couldn't remember when she'd laughed so much, and she delighted in having a witty sparring partner. This was a relaxed, charming side of him that she had only vaguely suspected, and she felt a sudden thrill, realizing how perfectly their humors complemented each other's. That was rare. She knew from the wicked way his eyes danced that he was enjoying himself, too.

She leaned against the counter, trying to give him room in the crowded space, and reached her wooden spoon in now and then to stir the noodles. They would invariably collide, until she suspected his ill-timed elbow wasn't always an accident. He simmered onions, peppers, tomatoes and garlic, and then added these to a pan of browned meat. With a can of tomato paste and a sampling of the spices in Claire's cupboard, it was nearly ready. Finally he drained the noodles and dumped everything together.

"But it's just goulash!" she declared.

"What?" he exclaimed, offended. "This is not ordinary goulash, my dear. This is the finest, most exotic, most enticing goulash—"

"'Enticing?'"

"Definitely enticing. Look at that. Could you resist it? This is really enticing stuff here."

The corners of his eyes were crinkling with merriness, and there was a flicker of something more. There is nothing as attractive as happiness, and she couldn't have resisted encouraging his smile if her life depended on it. They stood there with their spoons in the disorderly kitchen, completely at ease, and she wondered if they could possibly be the two people who had met over a flat tire a few nights before. It seemed years since then.

They set the little table, and rediscovered the cassette player. Raleigh had brought music, thinking she might like a change from the radio, and she sorted through the few tapes until she found one of Duke Ellington. They turned on the tape deck and sat down to an enticing dinner featuring Raleigh's Desert Delight, salad and wine. Jolly's heather and daisies presided.

They ate slowly, and although the goulash with its hint of curry was the best she had ever tasted, she kept getting absorbed in the conversation and forgetting to eat. He poured them each another glass of wine, and the light camaraderie jelled into something warmer. In the shadows, Raleigh's eyes took on a dark glimmer, and he watched her steadily.

"Tell me about your geology proposal. How much more do you need to do now?"

With the work she had completed that morning, she was finished as far as the research went, and with a little urging, she launched into a full description of what she had done. It came rushing out—all the sites she had visited and the ideas she had worked out during her three months. There had been no one to really understand and listen, and talking about it pulled some of the loose ends together in her own mind. The hours of solitude and lonely determination spoke volumes to someone who could read between the lines, and Raleigh listened keenly.

"And so," she summed up, "all I really need to do now is collect up my gear and double-check my notes, and then go write it up. My uncle will give me a corner of his office with a word processor so I can write up the report. It's enough work for a month, really, but I'm anxious to finish up, so I hope to be done three weeks from now. Beginning of April, I suppose."

He nodded, the blue of his eyes piercing from over his wineglass. His regard made her doubly aware of the loose neckline of her blouse, and she settled back in her chair. Even silent, he intrigued her, and she wished she knew about him, really. The tape reached the end and

clicked off, filling the room with silence and the hum of
things going to sleep outside. Gently, subtly, the tone of
the silence changed. Raleigh watched her, revealing a
puzzling fascination in the very arc of her arm upon the
table. Claire sensed it, uncertainly, knowing vaguely that
something was expected of her. Instinct told her one
thing; her past code of self-protection told her another.
She took the slight pause to summon her courage and
then, casually, she leaned on the table and ran her finger around her wineglass. She made her voice deliberately light.

"There's something I've wanted to ask, and it seems
almost absurd to ask it now, but I still don't know. Why
have you come to Death Valley?"

Ever so slightly, he stiffened. She knew immediately
she had chosen the wrong tack. He inhaled slowly, a
mocking gleam beneath his eyelids. He took a moment,
and then smiled quizzically. "I'm a photographer on
vacation. Visiting Sophie. No?"

Her stomach grew heavy with disappointment and
confusion. He knew she wasn't a fool, and yet he was
declaring his front for the cover it obviously was. They
hadn't known each other long, it was true, but she
thought they had grown to trust each other, and after
telling him of all her efforts and hopes, his answer was
little less than a slap in the face. She recoiled. Was she
mistaken about him entirely? Her finger took another
circle around the rim of her glass, and then, with an effort, she looked straight at him. She couldn't know how
the honesty and pain from those clear violet eyes would
haunt him. Now, what he saw caused him to reach forward and catch her hand from its perch on the glass. The
last of her wine spilled unnoticed on the tablecloth.

"Claire, you must trust me. There is something I can't tell you, for your own sake as well as mine."

He spoke urgently, standing now, and leaning across the table. They were very close.

"But why?" she whispered.

He drew her up so they were standing together, and his serious eyes looked through her as if searching her soul.

"I can only ask you to trust me."

For a long moment she looked into his strong face, wondering what his secret could be, and then she knew: she had to trust him. Infinitesimally, she nodded. Relief and wonder chased each other over his face, and then his arms were around her and he was kissing her. Insistent was the pressure of his body against hers, as they merged close in a promise that was long overdue. The heat of the first kiss carried through to the next, demanding; and then, wondrously, his touch became gentle, caressing. A warmth flushed her cheeks and stole through her whole being.

"Claire," he whispered, and pulled her next to him on the low couch. She slid willingly into his arms, running her hands over the chamois that covered his broad back. He touched her cheek with his thumb, and traced the line to her jaw as he had the day before, and after a delicious moment, his lips traced the same line. Claire felt her pulse thrill as his kiss found the hollow of her throat, and she moved closer to him still. He paused only to look again into her eyes, and when she answered his question with the softest of kisses, his passion took over again, filling them both with an intensity she had never known before.

She tangled her fingers in the shock of hair she had longed to touch, and closed her eyes in abandon. She had wanted this, craved to touch him and be touched in

return. Her last shyness was stripped away, left behind
with suspicion and doubt. His warm closeness touched
a need deep within her, a fundamental loneliness she
hadn't known she possessed. It was so simple, so overwhelming, that the conviction overrode her last lingering nervousness. This was right, the two of them
together like this, indulging the desires that had drawn
them together, fulfilling the dialogue that had raged beneath their everyday interaction. In the dawning wonder of it, she sought even closer intimacy, clasping him
tightly in a compelling embrace.

Their passion was fierce, like the dry winds of the desert floor, whipping the burning dust into a frenzy, suddenly, frighteningly, and then leaving every inch tingling
and changed as they eased away. They lay together in
warm disorder, and a gurgle of laughter welled up behind her smile.

"Happy?" he asked.

"This can't be my gullibility any longer. I think you
were onto something with the magic of—"

He interrupted her with another kiss, and she quickly
forgot what she had intended to say.

The chill against her hot arm was the first indication
she had that something was wrong. With an oath, Raleigh sat up, and they turned startled eyes to the doorway.

In it, with the night dark behind him, stood Harris
Dell. He carried a gift box and an ugly expression. His
surprise had not turned out the way he'd expected.

"Harris!" Claire exclaimed, trying clumsily to read-
just her blouse. Another gust of the cool night air shattered the last shreds of intimacy.

Raleigh was standing, silent and flushed, his emotion
contained in a tenseness pulled very fine. Bare-chested

and devil-eyed, he looked capable of mangling any-thing in his path. What Harris could only sense, Claire recognized fully, and she quickly began an introduc-tion, hoping to avert further trouble.

"Harris," she began more calmly. "This is Raleigh Durban. My supervisor, Harris Dell."

"You didn't tell me you were expecting company," Raleigh said, his voice laden with ice, and his eyes never leaving the intruder's face.

"I wasn't," she began. "I thought—"

"I thought I'd surprise you, Claire," said Harris. "Happy birthday and all that. You must have known I'd remember."

She knew nothing of the sort. He stepped into the trailer, and before she guessed what he was up to, he slid an arm around her shoulders and gave her a hug. His smile was a clear challenge to Raleigh, and before Claire could shrug him off and explain, Raleigh had stiffened even more, and stepped past them to the door.

"It was getting to be time to go, anyway," he said, re-trieving his shirt. "You won't be needing a chauffeur anymore."

With an ironic bow, he was gone.

"Raleigh, wait!" she called, shaking off Harris. There was no answer from the darkness and she spun back, livid.

"What do you think you're doing? Of all the nerve. Couldn't you even knock?"

Harris, handsome and blond, but no longer smiling, leaned past her and closed the door.

"I did knock. Several times. Apparently you didn't hear me."

"You're damn right I didn't hear," she said, blush-ing anew. "I mean—"

He laughed, a sour sound.

"No, I suppose not. I wouldn't have if I'd been so busy myself. We should have sent someone out long ago to help you with all your work. One might even say you've been overcome."

Her eyes narrowed to slits and she was dangerously close to slapping him.

"All right, I'm kidding. Let's not lose our tempers, after all. He ran out quick enough, and a girl shouldn't get all worked up over a little thing on her birthday."

"You are insufferable. How dare you, how dare you talk to me that way!" Her voice threatened to become shrill, and she couldn't stop it even if she had wanted to. "I'll excuse you only on the grounds you've been badly startled after a long journey. But I don't want to hear another word you have to say. Get out. Now."

He was startled, and for a second she had a crazy desire to laugh. She knew she had to get him out, and soon, because an even greater desire to bawl her head off was teasing the backs of her eyes.

"You're beside yourself. You don't know what you're saying. Why don't we sit down and—"

"No," she interrupted. "Get this through your head: I know what I'm saying, and I've asked you to leave. I'll talk to you in the morning, but right now I'm having a hard time not saying something that could get me fired."

He laughed, but the sound died unrequited. He looked at her, hard, and then stepped toward the door.

"Good night," he said quietly. "I'll see you for coffee at the restaurant at nine tomorrow."

He left her standing frozen in the middle of the room,

and as the door clicked shut behind him, she sat down on the couch that had offered paradise just moments before, and stared, dumbstruck, at the flowers on the table.

# Chapter Nine

Claire looked up from her coffee roll, and struggled to keep sheer amazement from her face. Harris was incredible, and she couldn't imagine how she hadn't noticed it when she'd been with him three months before. He was arrogant with the waitress, unnecessarily loud, and he had an irritating way of clicking his spoon inside his coffee cup. But his manners were just a beginning. Now he was smiling at her, oblivious to her cues of disapproval. Even when he was being friendly, his whole bearing was intolerable. She ducked her head down again and gathered her wits. To all purposes, this man was her employer, and it was with difficulty that she refrained from walking out in complete exasperation.

Little did she realize that across the table from her, Harris was experiencing very different sentiments. He found her more attractive than ever, and he was vaguely aware that having found her with another man made her all the more desirable, and proved her to be accessible.

Wicked thoughts flashed through his mind, interrupting his concentration and making his palms damp. They were sitting in an awkward pause when the waitress was pouring another cup of coffee, and they didn't want her to overhear their conversation. Claire poked at her coffee roll and Harris pushed his chair back just enough to make it scrape loudly against the floor. It could have been grating down her spine.

"Well, Mr. Dell, I think that just about covers everything," she said. "I'll leave the trailer keys with the ranger and you can send someone out for it. It'll take me a month to write up my thesis, but I'm sure you'll be satisfied with the results. I've been able to follow my proposal almost line by line, despite my recent injury."

"Yes," he said, with a sly little smirk. "I thought we might get around to that. When did I become Mr. Dell again, by the way? Perhaps it was the same time you found a chauffeur? Now don't get huffy. I've kept my ears open up at the hotel, my girl, and I can't say I admire your choice of companions. If you want to hang around with questionable persons, I should think you'd be a bit more discreet—if only as a representaive of our company."

She could feel her blood beginning to boil, and was getting a creepy feeling about the way his eyes wandered over her. This was rudeness of another sort, and she resented it.

"I think we'd better leave that remark alone, Mr. Dell. If I misled you before in any way, I beg your pardon; but I don't think that allows you to comment on my personal life now."

Harris shifted in his chair again and an ugly look replaced the roving one in his pale eyes. How could she have ever thought he was handsome? Never had she been so aware of how a person's character dictated the lines of their countenance.

"It doesn't, does it? Even putting aside my own interests . . . if you get us connected with the drug scandal that's brewing here, we'll stop your career dead in its tracks, no matter what the quality of your work."

"*What?* Drug scandal? I don't know what you're talking about, and how dare you say that about my work? I can't believe you."

She could feel the heat flooding her face, and a cold hand gripped her heart. There couldn't be any truth behind what he was implying. Just misinformed gossip up at the hotel. Harris was leaning back now, with one fist on the edge of the table. Leaning as he was, his neck looked narrow between the padded shoulders of his stylish coat. She knew she couldn't trust him three feet. Suddenly he leaned forward and exuded a sad earnestness, while his voice lost its depth.

"Forgive me, I had no right to say that. I don't actually have any proof and I never meant to threaten you anyway. It's just that I get jealous. You and I got along so well in December, and I've been looking forward to seeing you again. Then, seeing you with that guy's arms around you frustrated me more than I believed it could. Claire, I—I—"

He stopped, seeing her closed face. This last speech had disgusted her more than anything he had said yet, and she wondered at his inconsistency. It was so different from Raleigh's self-confident reticence, and she felt an ache as she thought again of his proud departure the night before. She should have sent Harris flying, and now she was listening to his lamentations. His desire gave her chills.

"Mr. Dell, I think enough has been said. If you still need to talk to me, you can call me at my uncle's in Chicago in a few days."

Without shaking the hand he desperately offered, she stood and walked out, shivering as she stepped into the clear sunlight. Slimy, she thought, and dangerous because he's just spineless enough to do something crazy. She vowed to get out of Death Valley and finish up all connections with Earthquakes, Inc. as soon as possible—even if it cost her that recommendation she'd been counting on.

She hurried into her car before Harris could come out of the restaurant, but she took her time getting back to the trailer park. The thought of entering her little home was loathsome to her. During the night she had fled, taking her coat and leaving the dinner dishes and the stifling atmosphere behind her. She had walked for hours on the golf course, watching the half-moon and fighting the feelings that threatened to overwhelm her. This morning, all of the day before seemed like some dream, and she had gotten up and left, barely noticing where she was. Now the door was before her, and she knew what she would find inside. She would either have to admit the worries and passion that were beating against the back of her brain, or walk like a zombie through the next days until she was on the plane home. Lifelessly, she fit the key in the lock. She would put everything on hold for as long as she could.

The first thing she saw as the door swung open was Raleigh's cassette player, where it had been left inconspicuously on the floor. Now it jumped into her sight as the only alien thing in the small space, and it had a curious effect upon her knees. She sat down on the couch and pulled the light machine toward her. Duke Elling-

ton was still inside, silent and sadly disturbing. She put
it away from her and then reached for it again. Slowly a
plan was filtering through her mind. This was his, and
he had clearly forgotten it. The loss of one tape deck
wasn't going to break his budget, even if he did remember it, and she knew, somehow, that he wouldn't come
knocking on her door looking for it. Not after what had
happened the night before, and the conclusions he must
have drawn from Harris's interruption. She had let him
leave with a huge misconception, but perhaps here was
the opportunity to clear it up. She would bring him his
tape deck, and get a chance to explain. In fact, she
shouldn't have to do much explaining at all. If she were
trusting him as she had promised, then he could at least
do the same for her. She could explain the connection
with Harris in two minutes flat.

She jumped up, once again ignoring the dirty dishes
and general disarray; there were more important things
to attend to. She ran to the bathroom, washed her face,
and with a hurried hand, brushed a smudge of color on
her lips and a wisp of black on her lashes. The makeup
bolstered her confidence, though at any other time it
would have been the last thing she needed to rely on.
Pallor fought with the tan her face had acquired, but she
didn't stop to notice. Within minutes she was racing to
the hotel, the tape deck beside her and a sweet hope beginning to sing in her anxious heart. They would clear
things up. They had to.

From the parking lot she could see two figures on the
terrace above, and immediately recognized Sophie. The
broad back could belong to no one else but Raleigh, and
she hurried up the stairs to the lobby. The reception desk
was empty, and she headed straight for the terrace when
she overheard their voices and stopped.

The breeze was coming in toward her, and she could see their sunlit shadows on the green tile floor. Never would she forget that bright, simple image on the patch of green between the open French doors, for the two forms came closer, hesitated and then merged into one silhouette.

"You're right, of course," came Sophie's voice. It was barely a whisper, and then it laughed softly. "You always were right, Ral. It's one of your charms, I suppose."

The forms drew even closer still, and Claire stood stupefied, an unhappy eavesdropper, until she turned away with tears brimming behind her lids. The cord slipped from her fingers and the plug of the cassette player landed on the polished wooden floor. In the silence, a pin drop would have sounded like a truck going by, and the plug was more than enough to draw the attention of the couple on the porch.

With a tanned hand still on Sophie's arm, Raleigh stepped back and looked into the lobby.

"Who's—?" Sophie asked, stepping forward too. She stopped, and the green eyes flashed at Claire before turning to Raleigh, who stood defiantly, staring at the intruder. Claire knew that particular look. He was mocking, challenging her.

She gritted her teeth, swallowed a sob and turned toward the desk. With a quick stride, she set the cassette player next to the registration book, and headed for the stairs. She caught herself on the banister as she nearly tripped, and then she couldn't get into her car fast enough.

She laughed bitterly to herself. So much for clearing everything up. Now I know his relationship with Sophie at least, she thought. And he won't need to buy a new tape deck. Her throat tightened dangerously as she flew toward the trailer park. And I was supposed to trust him.

She parked behind her trailer, turned off the ignition, leaned her head against the steering wheel and burst into tears. I love him, she thought. He's a cheat and a liar, and probably a drug dealer, and I love him so much my soul wants to scream. She clenched the wheel and buried her eyes into her knuckled fists. Tears came in silent sobs until she didn't care if she ever stopped. Through her misery, finally, the sound of a guitar from the far side of the trailer lot penetrated gently. It was a mournful, searching sound. A bearded fellow was picking next to his motorcycle. Claire sniffed and looked over at him, wiping her tears on the back of her hand. She was drained, emotionally exhausted, and she keyed in on the musician, until a numbness settled her nerves.

Whatever happened to the strong, sassy woman you used to be? she asked herself sadly. Where is the spunk, and humor and courage? This is not the end of the world. This is a three-day romance with a guy who turns out to be a toad instead of a prince; nothing to lose your head about.

She wasn't convincing herself. She wanted to sit in the Scout forever, but the habit of practicality wouldn't let her. She stepped out, and waved to the guitarist. He nodded, and concentrated again on his pick.

That afternoon went by in a daze for Claire. She cleaned up the trailer, packed some boxes and brought them to the post office to be mailed to Chicago. She used the phone there to arrange a flight out of Las Vegas the next day, and then swung by the store for what promised to be her last can of soup. Each time she made an errand, she hoped and dreaded that she might see Raleigh. Celebrating her finish was the last thing she felt like doing, and she even wondered if she could leave the next day without seeing Jolly. That would be too inconsiderate, she knew, but she decided to put off the goodbye until as late as possible. She didn't want her friend to see her unhappiness. She had returned to her trailer for the fourth time that day and was sorting her photos when Jolly herself scratched on the screen of the back window.

"Claire? Are you in, honey?"

Jolly's funny, musical voice almost brought on Claire's tears again, and she hurried to the doorway to meet her. She could see immediately that something was wrong with Jolly, and she reached out a hand to steady her as she stepped in.

"Claire. There you are. I told you something was going on. Where's your man?"

Claire blushed, and started to stutter out a denial, when Jolly interrupted.

"You don't know. I can see you don't know. What a relief you just gave this old heart. Claire, that boy's in trouble. There's a plane coming in tonight with a load of the real thing and everybody who doesn't have an alibi will be answering a lot of questions tomorrow. You come over to the house with me and Juan, and if you don't want to say anything about your man, you don't have to say a word. We'll never let on."

Claire felt the cold clutch at her heart and spread like liquid helium through her veins. A drug plane, and Raleigh might be involved. She gripped Jolly's arm and nearly shook her.

"You've got to tell me, Jolly. What do you know about this plane? Where is it coming in?"

Jolly's eyes narrowed, and then she shook her head. Her usual sparkle was entirely gone, revealing the strong, life-toughened woman beneath.

"I try to tell you, Claire. I try. A fling is one thing, but you've got to be able to see when to get out. Your man has been running with a shady crowd ever since he got here. I hoped I was wrong, and I thought he couldn't be as bad as it looked because you were with him, but now we know. That man's poison."

Claire backed away from her, not understanding what she was hearing. The cold was reaching her fingers now, and she fought it from numbing her brain with fear.

"What are you telling me?"

"You can't do anything."

"Tell me!" Claire said, sitting down with weak knees, her lifelessness replaced by desperation.

"The plane's landing on the playa tonight. He didn't tell you anything? They try this every few months, and usually they get busted. I've still got relatives over the border and we hear things. Your man's been setting up a big deal, but it seems the authorities, who were supposed to be gone, have heard about it, and they're going to catch it. There's nothing you can do, Claire. I tell you. The plane's well on its way by now, and the dealers and the rangers will be hiding from each other in the hills."

There was a silence. He had asked her to trust him, and despite the evidence of his kiss with Sophie that afternoon, she had been sure that even if he'd deceived her, he couldn't be involved with something illegal. She knew now that a part of her had still been hoping.

"I thought for sure you knew," Jolly said gently.

"I've been alone at my sites, day after day," Claire said, "or else I've been with Raleigh. Perhaps I refused to see. Even Harris knew this morning that something was up. How could he?''

"It has been in the air for a couple weeks now. Many people speculate, but nobody has proof or details. Juan and I are probably the only ones in town who actually know it is planned for tonight. Besides the authorities, that is, and how they heard is a puzzle.''

"Then how do you know Raleigh is involved? Maybe you've made a mistake. Maybe... He's probably having dinner with Sophie right now!''

Jolly watched her with troubled eyes, and reached out a hand to quiet her.

"I wish it were so, honey. But I know it is not.''

She spoke with the simplicity of informed conviction. Claire's mind leveled to a dull void. Jolly had to be wrong. The only way was to see Raleigh.

"I have to go," she said quietly, standing up and looking around her absently. "I have to find him, Jolly," she repeated, and her words gave her the assurance she needed. That was all there was to it.

Jolly looked at her, and her sad face broke into an even sadder smile.

"You don't know what you're doing, little honey. I try to tell you, I try, but you young ones never know.''

Slowly, she turned and stepped down from the trailer. With the grace of a queen, she turned to look at Claire once more.

"Good luck," she whispered, and then moved off into the evening grayness.

Raleigh wasn't at the hotel, and the receptionist didn't know when he would be back. With an anxious heart, Claire headed for the ranger station. Mr. Ecks might be able to help and she could trust him, even if she had to depend on personal loyalties that transcended the law.

She pulled the Scout up before his home just as the last daylight was snuggling against the horizon, and she was relieved to see lights on inside. If he was here, at least he wasn't already busting drug planes on the playa. She hurried to the door and stood waiting while the bell rang inside. A bulb came on over the door.

"Hi, Claire. Come on in."

He left her, for the phone was ringing, and he stepped into the other room to answer it. His voice was a mumble through the doorway as she stepped around a paper-strewn table to take a look at a map on the wall. Every canyon was carefully marked, some with notes and dates. Quickly she looked for Racetrack Valley, where the playa was located. It wasn't very far, as the bird flies, but as she started adding up the mileage, she realized with despair that it was a good hour-and-a-half away. She could never be there in time to save Raleigh.

She had not wanted to believe Jolly, but she could no longer disregard the evidence she had herself. He had admitted that visiting Sophie was a cover. He had met twice in her presence with suspicious-looking men who then vanished, and both times he had created a diversion to distract any attention the meetings might have aroused. That she had been used as a cover herself was only a touch on the pain she was beginning to feel. Then there were all his inexplicable hesitations, his watchfulness, the gas he had gone through and all the unusual places he had visited. Now there was Jolly's story and his absence from the hotel. Even Harris had heard something. Most of all was the very request he had made that she trust him. Whatever he was mixed up in was something he couldn't even tell her. Somehow that hurt most of all. She knew they could never have the relationship that had been growing, but she would have risked what she could to warn him to get clear of his drug deal.

Mr. Ecks returned from the other room. He didn't seem surprised to see her there; in fact, she almost felt he had been expecting her.

"That was the call we've been waiting for. It's just what we expected. Bill has the helicopter ready, so I'm on my way. We'll tell you about it later."

Claire didn't know what he was saying. He obviously thought she knew more than she did, but on the other hand, she didn't know how much he knew. Who was included in the "we" he had mentioned. Perhaps just the other authorities, she thought. She desperately wanted to know whether Raleigh was involved, but she couldn't ask, because if he didn't know, she didn't want to tell. She had to know what was happening.

"Couldn't I come with you?" she asked. "I wouldn't get in the way, and I, I—I wouldn't get in the way."

"Ridiculous. Far too dangerous."

He headed for the door.

"Mr. Ecks!" Claire pleaded.

He turned, and she summoned her courage to ask the question. He spoke before she got the chance, and his voice was unexpectedly gentle.

"He'll be taken with the rest. I'm sorry, Claire. There won't be a chance to talk to him."

He had guessed! Her knees loosened and she steadied herself with a hand on the table.

"That's not it," she denied. "Please, you have to take me."

Mr. Ecks frowned, but her eyes were more eloquent than her words had been.

"Please," she urged.

For an instant he hesitated, and then he nodded abruptly. Claire caught her breath.

"You mustn't blame me if it's ugly," he said.

The words slit through her. He must want her to see so that she could believe the worst. Maybe the shock would make it easier to get over him. And maybe, just maybe, she could still do something. At least she would be there to see.

An elderly man who looked familiar to Claire stuck his head in the door. He hesitated when he saw her, and looked at Mr. Ecks.

"It's okay, Bill. Miss Bennett is coming with us. Let's go."

Bill took another look at Claire, and then they hurried out. The night had gotten cool, and a heavy half-moon was low in the sky. Claire sniffed the evening air, and sat between the two silent men as they drove to the landing strip. A helicopter was already lit up and whirring, and they ran under the wind into the cockpit. A man jumped out and his mouth formed "Good luck" before he ran off. Bill ran his hand over the controls and then, with a heavy sway to the right, they were up and soaring over the mountains.

A violet blanket covered everything below them, and the engine hummed loudly, hushing the voices of the two men in the front seats. Claire huddled next to her window, watching the eerie shadows glide by beneath her. Everything was so stark and bleak. There was none of the welcome she had come to know. Instead, the barren peaks and empty canyons were grimly surreal. She shivered, pulling her jacket closer and gripping it until her knuckles shone in the dim light.

Mr. Ecks leaned back to see how she was doing.

"These guys are pretty clever, aren't they?" he yelled over the roar.

She gulped back a sob and nodded dismally. Perhaps this was a mistake. She should never have come.

He turned back, satisfied, and they all watched for the playa to appear below them. Ahead and slightly to the left, it gleamed dully in the moonlight, an expanse of clay lake-bottom, baked shiny and cracked by the sun and winds. It was utterly flat, a refuge among the rough peaks and hills. They didn't approach too closely, for they didn't want to be detected from the ground. They landed in Hidden Valley, one low range east of Racetrack Valley, where two other helicopters had already landed and several men were talking in small groups. A car was waiting for them, and they drove over the bumpy road until they neared the playa. No one spoke, as if they were hushed by the urgency of their errand. They dimmed the lights and continued on, slowly, making as little sound as possible. Then they drove off the road, left the car and walked quickly the rest of the way.

Mr. Ecks put his arm around her shoulders and led her to where a group of men was hiding at the base of one of the hills.

"You'll be safe here. Stick with Bill if anything gets out of hand. I'm already regretting that I brought you, so please be careful."

He gave her a quick hug, and then slipped off into the night. Claire shivered again and looked toward the playa, letting her eyes get used to the distance and trying to imagine what it was like in daylight. Now it was a deadly quiet flatness, stretching down the valley as far as she could see and glowing dimly with reflected moonlight. An island of rocks bulged out of it at the near end, diminished by the distance, but nonetheless stark and black. The hills around them were still. Fingers of fear and anxiousness danced down the back of her neck. Raleigh was somewhere out there.

She thought she could hear something behind her, and she glanced quickly at Bill. He nodded reassuringly, as if to say "They're with us." Two men weren't ten feet behind her, but she could barely tell they were there. She turned her head and strained to hear better, and every now and then she caught the briefest wink of cigarette red. Apparently these men had waited here before.

"Yep, that's right. 'S tough to do, but if you make a good flight through, you make more money in two days than you and I make in three years."

"Where's this drop from?" another voice whispered.

"The usual. They've got poppy fields in the Sierras, western Mexico. There are no roads back there mostly, but even so, the authorities really cracked down. Now the top-quality stuff is harder to get, and worth a lot more. It takes really tough guys. Shrewd guys. They're ruthless, too. No morals."

"You're telling me!" the other voice whispered back. "A couple years back I was in a bar down by the border when some of them shot a guy up with some sixty-four percent stuff and he ODed right there. I never did hear what they did with the body. That was before I joined the force."

The first man stifled a chuckle.

"Sure it was. They probably bribed you to look the other way."

The other one cursed, and the language was oddly out of place at such a low volume. Claire heard a muffled slap on a khakied knee, and they hushed into silent laughter.

"You know I'm not one of those types, you turkey. Lord, one of these days I'm going to take you seriously and then—"

The first man stopped him, and Claire turned to see him pointing, his arm a vague form. She looked in the direction it indicated, and there, sure enough, was a black, metallic, angular shape. It was so quiet she doubted for a second whether it was really a plane. It could more easily have been a giant, carnivorous bird, swooping low, looking for prey. It lowered below the line of the hills and she lost sight of it for a second. It was landing without a control tower, without a designated runway, without a light even indicating the way. It was the most daring thing Claire had ever seen, and she held her breath, expecting any second for the night to be blasted by the light of a crash.

Then suddenly the plane was rolling toward them, and a green light flashed once from the island of rocks. The hills remained still, and as she scanned them she saw no one. Were the police really there, or were the traffickers going to get away with this, after all? A moment later, she began to fear they hadn't seen the plane land.

A jeep pulled out from an invisible crevice just to the right of Claire and headed toward the plane. It must have been there the whole time, not two hundred feet away, and she hadn't known. She turned quickly around, but the small group behind her had seen it also, and the men were beginning to edge away from the slope. She was left with Bill, sitting against a rock like one of the clumps of sage.

On the playa, the jeep had reached the plane, and a couple of men had run out from the island of rocks. They were unloading the plane with startling efficiency, wasting no motion and making no noise. Claire couldn't believe this was really happening. When were the police going to do something?

Suddenly the playa was splayed with light. High beams of cars were directed on the plane, and the men there froze in midaction.

"Nobody move!" yelled a megaphone. One man started to run for the darkness, but the sound of a pistol shot stopped him. The noise echoed down the valley, while a party of police crept carefully across the playa. From her place on the hill, Claire could hear one of the men curse fiercely as the police surrounded them and moved in.

Behind her, Bill had gotten up, and he beckoned her to follow him.

"No," she said. "I have to see who's down there."

He hesitated, and then started down the slope with her in the direction of the lights. They reached the flat of the playa and she quickened her pace. Maybe he wasn't there. Maybe if Jolly had heard of the bust, so had Raleigh. Maybe this was some huge mistake, some hideous farce. She started to run, and could hear Bill's footsteps beside her. The distance was agonizingly farther than it looked, and she had to stop running before she reached the circle of police. In a glance, she saw the packages of heroin, the glint of the handcuffs as the police swarmed the dealers, and the little plane with its hatch open. An enormous spotlight, which was stronger than the combined headlights, pinned each object and person to a sharp shadow, as in a nightmare or horror film. Bill was talking to her, telling her to come back, but she didn't hear him. She was desperately searching the forms of the criminals. She had to find Raleigh, and yet she frantically hoped he wouldn't be there.

He was leaning against the jeep. An officer stood next to him and another man who was shaking his head and swearing to himself. Raleigh's jean jacket was jerked oddly on his shoulder, and his hands were cuffed behind him, while his gaze was concentrating on the plane. His hair was disheveled, but his eyes were bright in his dark face. Claire followed his gaze to the aircraft, hardly caring anymore what she saw. A huge man was being frisked against the plane, while another policeman covered him with a gun. As the frisker pinned the man's hands behind him and clicked handcuffs on his wrists, he struggled briefly and then spun around.

"When I find out which one of you talked," he began in a hateful tone, "I swear you'll wish you'd never been born." The other dealers looked at him and each other, but said nothing. The big man swore, and would have elaborated on what he was going to do to the traitor, but the sheriff took his arm and started moving him toward the cars.

"You'll never get the chance, Clem. There's enough evidence here to put you away for years," the sheriff said.

Claire felt cold with fear. Raleigh was one of these men. He was probably just as cruelly hardened. He couldn't be the same man she had come to know; it was impossible. But he was still leaning against the jeep, his proud profile silent against the moonlight. She took a step toward him, and then another, but he still didn't turn his head. She stood for a moment then, with the sad bitterness weighing heavily on her heart.

"And I was supposed to trust you," she said, her voice low, and thick with pain.

He flinched, and turned sharply toward her. His face paled to a ghastly gray, and his gaze stretched out to her, piercing her to the core.

"Claire," he whispered in an agonized croak.

But she couldn't bear to look at him anymore. She turned blindly and ran. How could he do this! Her mind reeled against the awful truth, and her heart set in a deadly ache.

She stumbled on the playa, and Bill caught her arm. He slowed her down, and walked next to her in the long beams of light, back to the cars.

He led her to a seat, and he himself took the driver's place. Mr. Ecks turned from a group of men, and crossed over to her window. He leaned his elbow on the roof and smiled at her.

"Really clever, like I said. Raleigh's the devil himself in disguise, don't you think?"

Never had his wit been so out of place. Claire flinched at his sarcastic admiration, and turned stricken eyes to his face. Instantly he was concerned.

"Take her back right away, Bill," he said. "Straight to her trailer. Get some sleep, Claire. Everything looks better in the morning. I knew I shouldn't have let you come. Promise me you'll forget it. Just forget the whole thing."

He waved them on, and the other cars let them by. She stared unseeing out the window into the darkness. She kept imagining the brightly lit commotion behind her, and Raleigh caught up in the middle of it. At the thought of his profile, so proud despite his arrest, she raised her hand to her eyes as if to erase the image. But it wouldn't vanish. It was the longest drive of her life, and she sat, hardly breathing the whole way, numbed to stone.

## Chapter Ten

Michigan Avenue was swathed in a drizzly cold, the kind that snuck into the bones and felt more like January than almost-April. Claire Bennett waited for the stoplight to change and moved with the crowd across the street. It had snowed the day before, and now, gray slush brimmed the edge of her sneakers and spattered the bottoms of her jeans. She was in a foul mood, and relished it. A tall shoulder brushed past her and hurried ahead, and she felt a spasm of emotion until she saw that the man's hair was merely brown, not raven black.

"This can't go on like this," she whispered aloud.

For ten days she had been more dead than alive, waking each day to hurry to her uncle's office before she could start thinking. In a tiny room off the main hallway, she was set up with a bookshelf, a desk and a word processor. Her little cousin had lent her his Barrel of Monkeys, and this sat behind the empty coffee mugs and dried-up pens. The room had been a haven, the only place where she found some relief from the thoughts that haunted her everywhere else, and she had thrown herself into her work as if a hundred demons were chasing her behind her back. Harris had called once to apologize, and she had listened to him quietly, no longer able to be offended or flattered by his persistence. She had promised to deliver her project within three weeks and, driven as she was, it looked as if it would only take her two.

The days passed quickly, without a break. She often worked through lunchtime, forgetting to eat, and looked up at the clock only as it was almost time to leave. Page after page of the report came out of the printer, each letter crisp and fresh, but the ruin it left behind was something she didn't see. In vain did her uncle try to get her to go out, or even just to take some time off. She felt, on the contrary, that she had far too much time when she wasn't busy.

"But my partners are beginning to think I don't feed you properly," he joked. "I knew we shouldn't have let you go out there on your own. Who knows what could have happened? Drug deals, snakes, flash floods. You could have gotten lost or attacked by a wild sheep, or—"

"Burros, Uncle Chaz, not sheep," she groaned. "And as you can see, I wasn't attacked by anything. I'm here, aren't I? I made it, didn't I?"

He nodded reluctantly, and continued to look skeptical.

"I suppose you did, although I'm not sure something didn't happen to you there. If you can think of anything I can do for you..."

He was getting red in the face and his deep voice was gruff with kindness and concern. Claire dreaded having him feel sorry for her. She forced herself to laugh, and reassured him that she was fine.

The evenings in her uncle's home were warm and welcoming. Little Jeremy, the surprise of her aunt and uncle's late middle age, amused her with stories of his rock collection and the salamander team. No, Jeremy didn't know what a salamander really was. He and his buddies made it up, and all he knew was that they did a lot of slithering in the halls and drove the teachers crazy. Aunt Betty would laugh and Claire would smile, and sooner or later Jeremy would put his little hand on her knee and ask why she was so sad. Aunt Betty would shoo him away and tell Claire not to mind him, but her gently concerned eyes asked the same question in a different way. Her aunt and uncle had always respected her reticence, and Claire had never been more thankful. But each day, she knew they worried more.

Claire would retire to the guest room and read or do extra research until she couldn't keep her eyes open. Then, in bed with the sheets pulled up under her chin, she would watch the shadows on the ceiling until the tears came. Every car hushing by in the night street would swell her despair, as in her half-sleeping imagination she'd believe it might be Raleigh coming for her somehow. Later, she would fall into an uneasy sleep, and wake to hurry off to her little office once again, more exhausted and determined than the morning before.

She stood now before a cookie store, looking in at the large hot disks and leaning close so her breath fogged the window. Today was Aunt Betty and Uncle Chaz's twenty-seventh wedding anniversary, and they were throwing a little party. They had insisted they didn't want a gift, but she had wanted to find something—not anything big, but a token of love and thanks. They had

been like parents to her, and now they were caring for
her as if she were one of their own when she was in
trouble. It was the least she could do.

A woman inside slid a new pan of hot cookies onto a
shelf, and Claire followed another customer into the
shop. She bought a diverse dozen of the cookies, smiling at their ridiculous names and absorbing the exaggerated friendliness of the salesclerks. They were all slim,
high-school-age kids, and they clearly took advantage of
a job where the manager let them goof around now and
then. They had so much life, it seemed, and it exhausted Claire just to be close to it. When had she aged
so much? She stepped into the evening just as a light
drizzle began to fall. The hot bag warmed her hands and
she hurried the rest of the way to the Loop, where she
caught the subway home.

In a train full of glum people, she happened to sit
across from an elderly couple who were holding hands
and whispering like a pair of lovebirds. The balding man
was carrying a large, bulky sack that held something soft
like a pillow, and judging from their conversation, they
had used it as an excuse to go shopping together. Claire
didn't know why they brought a lump to her throat. Why
did everyone have somebody, she wondered, and when
had it ever bothered her so much that she didn't?

Heavens, Claire, she scolded herself. You've absolutely fallen into a decline. When did you get to be so
poetic? She couldn't believe herself, but she doubted she
would ever revert to her old, practical self. Her soul had
changed; it was the result of knowing someone, and
learning to really love him. She couldn't help it if she'd
been jolted into full life. She shook her head, but the
thoughts kept coming.

That next morning she had risen early, packing the remainder of her belongings and locking up the trailer for the last time. She had waited as long as she dared for some news or a message of some kind, though she didn't know who would send one. At last she had gone to say goodbye to Jolly and her husband. Jolly had given her a huge, enveloping hug and three pounds of dates.

"You will get through this, Claire, and some day you will be passing through this valley again and you and I will laugh over the times we have had."

Her eyes had already begun to gleam again; and her humor refused to be subdued.

"We'll paint the town red, you and me. Juan won't know what's happened to us and the next thing you know we'll be a famous tourist attraction all by ourselves."

Her infectious chuckle followed, succeeding as usual in making even the unfunniest things amusing. Claire had left, smiling and promising to write, and as she had stepped onto the plane in Las Vegas later, she had held on to her vision of Jolly as the one wholly good memory of her three months in Death Valley. Everything else—Harris, the project, and finally Raleigh—they had all turned the most promising time of her life into a series of disillusionments.

That flight to Chicago had seen the beginning of bitterness and confusion that had been more than she thought she could stand. Since then, the edge of her that contained anger and pain had given her the drive to plunge into her work, and everything else was an effort to keep thoughts of Raleigh from her mind.

She stepped off the subway and walked the three blocks home, while the drizzle turned to true-blue rain and the cookies lost their warmth. She arrived soaked, cold and tired, to find her aunt bustling about in a bright apron and laying out coffee cups. She and Jolly would have been kindred spirits.

"Cookies! You wretch." A beaming smile contradicted the insult, and Claire knew she had chosen correctly. "You got a letter. Do you think you could give me a hand when you get cleaned up? Goodness, I'm never ready for these things, and is Chaz anywhere to be seen, I ask you? No. It's there on the radiator by the stairs, and tell Jeremy to get out of the laundry when you get up. I can hear him up there."

She whirled back into the kitchen, and Claire accorded her a half smile as she picked up the letter and started up. It was from Jolly, and she was interrupted from opening it by a thud in the laundry room.

"Jeremy?" she called.

There was no reply, and she stepped into the hall and leaned in the doorway.

"What are you doing?"

Jeremy had dumped a load of clean clothes onto the floor and was crouched over with the basket upside down on his back. His shock of brown hair was standing up with static and his pink cheeks had mischief written all over them.

"I'm a turtle!" he crowed, and laughing, he toppled over on his side in the clothes. Claire growled and jumped in to tickle him. The boy shrieked and giggled, pushing her hands with his fat little fingers, and leaning his head back in sheer glee. Her heart lightened for the first time in weeks, and a real smile softened her face. Finally Jeremy sat up, and when he looked at her, he put a finger to her cheek.

"There, you're happy. Should I do the turtle again?"

She laughed.

"No, you monster. Your mom needs some help so let's go see what we can do."

She changed out of her wet things, and they trooped down the stairs together. Betty smiled to see them. For the next hour, they were all busy, and then they ran up to put on their company clothes. Claire was still slipping into her dress when the doorbell rang, and she heard Betty's startled cry and then her peremptory voice telling Jeremy to go open the door. The first of the guests chatted amiably with Jeremy until Betty ran down and rescued him. Claire brushed her hair back from her face. She had decided she liked the added length, and the hairdresser had agreed, so she had just shaped it. With her tan fading too, Claire thought she now looked just like everyone else. Even if she didn't, nobody who mattered would be there to see her tonight. A twinkle looked back at her from the mirror, and she smiled. You're pushing it a little too far, aren't you? she scolded. She went down to help her aunt, resolved to have a good time. Soon the living room was full of comfortable, middle-aged men and women, the sort who like to settle in a couch and stay there for a while. They were mostly colleagues from the furniture business, and all good friends. They greeted Claire and made themselves at home, and joked about Chaz being late to his own party.

Betty laughed too, but Claire could see her aunt was concerned about her husband. It was like him to be late, but not this late.

A long half-hour had gone by since the first guest had arrived, and finally they heard a key in the lock. Claire turned to see her uncle come in, and behind him came another, slender man. As he stepped into the light and adjusted his glasses, she stared at him in wonder, for it

was no other than Jake Bowing, the astronomer from
Death Valley.

What's he doing here? she thought. And then: maybe
he knows something about Raleigh. From a stricken
pale, her face suddenly flushed with color, and she
stepped forward shyly to greet him. Jake had seen her
the instant the door opened, and he thought, objec-
tively, that he had never seen her look more lovely.

"Claire," he said softly, taking her hand in both of
his. Claire blushed all the more, feeling her uncle's gaze
upon them. The big man chuckled.

"This friend of yours met me at the office and he
wouldn't leave me alone until I invited him to come on
over and see you himself. Since I hadn't gotten a present for Betty, I figured any surprise would be better than
nothing."

He threw a saucy grin to his wife and Betty laughed
back. The two of them exchanged looks, and Chaz
shrugged, jerking his head toward his niece. She was still
so stunned to see Jake that she hardly heard what was
going on; but the company was off on the right track
now, and with Chaz spreading his good mood wherever
he slapped a shoulder, it would have been impossible for
anyone not to have a good time. Claire put Jake's coat
in the closet, and the two of them snuck off to the
kitchen.

"I am so surprised to see you here," she said, gesturing him to a chair, which he didn't take.

"I had to see you, for a number of reasons. You are a
tricky person to locate. Did you know that nobody in
Death Valley knows your address? I couldn't believe it.
I hope you don't mind me intruding like this. When I

finally found your uncle, he was so friendly. He seemed to think you might be glad to see me."

He stopped, watching her, but only mild bewilderment presented itself on her face. Jake gave a rueful smile and shrugged.

"I thought that was a little much to expect. Perhaps your uncle confused me with someone else."

His meaning was clear to her now, and the ebbing color flooded up under her eyes once again. She reached a hand and set it on his sleeve.

"Jake, I am glad to see you. You must know I am. I think you and I would have been well on the way to being fast friends by now if we'd had more time together. I mean that sincerely."

At her slight emphasis on the word "friends" he gave his funny smile again, and sat down on the chair she had offered.

"Sure, Claire. I expect we can go ahead and consider ourselves buddies in any case." He smiled warmly this time. "There was another reason I came to see you, and I won't even try to be subtle or noble about it. I've been sent. I can't say I delight in playing the spy for someone else, but I owe Sophie a favor. Besides, I'm being very up-front and you don't have to tell me a thing if you don't want to."

Claire sat down opposite him, now truly confused. What could Sophie want to know about her, and why couldn't she ask it herself if it was so important? She smoothed the tablecloth along the edge of the table and readjusted a sprig of sage in a little dry bouquet that sat next to the salt and pepper.

"I'm not really sure what you want me to say," she began. "I don't know why she couldn't ask me whatever it is straight out—unless of course she doesn't want to write. I got the feeling she wasn't exactly fond of me."

He chuckled appreciatively.

"That's putting it mildly. I think she gives you full credit for stealing Raleigh away from her, though of course she would never say so. Instead she sends me to find out if you're still seeing him or whether she can do some coercing somewhere. Devious woman. She and I could get along awfully well if she weren't such a snake."

"Jake! What a thing to say."

"I'm kidding. You know I am. She and I go way back—even pre-Raleigh—and I actually think we might make a go of it if she ever gets him out of her system. We're an odd pair, but she needs me more than she realizes. That's another reason why I didn't mind doing her errand so much."

There was a pause, and they could hear Jeremy's piercing laughter high over the other voices of the party. Jake crossed his arms and settled back in his chair, looking at her with a quizzical smile, as if to say "so?"

"I don't know why I should hesitate," she began in a low, bitter voice. "I haven't heard a thing from him since he was arrested, and I don't expect to. I don't know how I could have been so mistaken about him, but I thank my lucky stars, my lucky—" She had to stop, for a thick lump in her throat was threatening to suffocate her. She stood up quickly and turned her back to him as she moved to the sink. She was viciously turning the faucet for a glass of water when Chaz stepped through the swing door.

"You folks okay out here?" he asked.

Claire faced him and gave an unconvincing smile.

"We're okay. We'll come out in a few minutes."

"No need to hurry," he said in a boisterous voice. His very presence was heartening. He gave them a blow-by-blow of Jeremy's wooing of one elderly guest, and at the same time poured a jug of apple cider into a glass pitcher. In a second he was gone, leaving the door rocking gently on its hinges as if after a fresh wind.

Claire could feel a prickle behind her eyelids, but the tears had been momentarily put on hold. Why was the thought of him so painful? But Jake was looking at her strangely, and seemed to be reconsidering something. He contemplatively rubbed the back of his fingers against his lower lip, and then he sniffed.

"You say you haven't heard from him since he was arrested? But how do you know he was arrested?"

She slammed her cup onto the table and sat.

"How do I know? I was there. I saw him, with his hands cuffed and the police about to drag him away."

Jake slowly shook his head.

"It doesn't make any sense to me. If you say you saw it, then you did, but I never heard anything about it and I would have. The day after you left, Sophie called up in a pouting mood, saying Raleigh had gone back to New York, and would I help her get rid of her guests. Naturally, there was nothing I could do, and she got mad, and then I didn't hear from her until three days ago."

He thought for a minute more, and then shook his head.

"But I'm sure I'd have heard if Raleigh was arrested. The whole area buzzed with the news from the drug bust, and I got a personal account of the whole thing from Mr. Ecks."

He was thinking aloud, and without wanting to doubt her, it was clear from the question in his eyes that he was perplexed and hadn't heard about either her or Raleigh being at the playa that horrible night. A wild hope sprang into her heart. Could it have been some cruel twist of her imagination? Had she not really seen what she had? And if Raleigh had been in New York, did it mean—?

"Jake," she said, with urgency making her low voice resonate, "tell me what Mr. Ecks told you."

He thought for a second and then, in a few concise sentences, he told the story exactly as she had seen it, but omitting entirely anything having to do with her or Raleigh. She was stunned. Had Mr. Ecks forgotten she flew with him in the helicopter? Had Bill forgotten too? It was preposterous.

"Something has upset you," Jake observed. "I don't know what it could be. If Raleigh told you he was messed up with the law, it was an unnecessarily complicated way to avoid you. Unlike him, too. He's always been very blunt with Sophie."

She shook her head, unable to order the wild thoughts that were racing through her mind.

"Tell me, Jake," she asked, "was it really all that hard to find me? I mean, did it take very long?"

He would have liked to comfort her, erase the strain around her eyes, but he smiled casually, and obediently answered the question.

"I thought it would be a cinch, because so many people in Death Valley liked you. I was sure one of them would know your address, but one said 'Cincinnati,' and one said 'Cleveland,' and the rest all said 'Back East,' as if that were specific enough."

Claire gave a thin smile, and he went on.

"Then I tried Earthquakes, Inc., or whatever it's called. At first they were uncooperative. I talked to some guy who asked me all sorts of suspicious questions before he'd help me out. I guess they have security reasons."

"I guess," she agreed.

Harris, of course. He'd be jealous of anyone, and enjoy using his authority to slow things up. He had eventually given the information, though. Couldn't Raleigh have gotten it too? Why hadn't he come, or called?

Jake was watching her closely, and he thought he understood. His glasses couldn't conceal the pity in his gentle eyes, and it brought Claire's tears closer to the edge. Impulsively, she reached across the table toward him.

"You know something, don't you?" she asked.

She spoke with quiet restraint, and he admired her pride. Jake was one to recognize strength, and inwardly he cursed Raleigh for causing her such pain.

"No," he said at last. "I don't know anything. I wish I could encourage you, and I wish I could vouch for Raleigh, but I can't."

A final thread twisted within Claire and held taut, suspended, and she concentrated as if she'd shatter the moment it snapped. She couldn't answer Jake. She didn't even want to try, and she wished for nothing more than to rush up to her room and think. Betty knocked, and then came in. Jake stood up and introduced himself.

"Your husband didn't explain that Claire and I were friends out in the desert, and I wouldn't have intruded if he had explained you were having an anniversary party. Congratulations."

Betty smiled and chattered like a cricket, throwing concerned glances over to Claire whenever she had to stop to catch her breath. From her rosy cheeks and the gleam in her eye, Claire quickly realized that her aunt had been sipping something besides cider, and as another cork popped in the living room, she knew why. Jake caught her eye, and although he kept his face serious, Claire knew he had understood, too.

"I tell you what," he said, when he could get a word in. "I'll drop by the next time I'm in Chicago again, and we can have a real chat. You have a delightful niece, Mrs. Bennett, and a very fortunate husband."

Betty was momentarily dumbfounded, and then with a courteous smile and the hint of a hiccup, she thanked Jake and went to look for his coat. Jake and Claire stood looking at each other, and then he put out his hand.

"I'm sorry we haven't gotten the chance to know each other better, but if there's ever anything I can do for you, I hope you'll let me know."

The thanks in her eyes gave his heart a last little ache, and then he dismissed his mild infatuation in exchange for friendship. Claire sensed his resolution, and gave him a hearty hug. Within minutes, he was walking down the cold, wet sidewalk with his coat hunched up around his ears, and Claire's heart was tugging inside her, not for the man, but for the news he had brought her.

She slowly closed the door, and moved back into the party. One look at the merry people was enough to convince her that this was not where she wanted to be. Little Jeremy was looking excited and tired at the same time, and was standing one-legged and close to his father. Claire beckoned to him from the doorway, and he gladly came over to her.

"These people are really nice," he said, his big eyes blue and happy. "Don't you like them?"

Claire took another look around the living room. The younger partner of the business was standing next to his wife. This man had once asked her to marry him, and

she had almost offended her uncle irrevocably by not
accepting. That seemed like years ago, but it could only
have been a couple. How bitter she had been then, and
how indifferent now. Would this happen to her present
feelings as well? The man was already tiring of flaunting the new wife at his side. She was a mousy thing, with
a heavy, inappropriate necklace weighing down her
chest. The looks she turned on her husband were ador-
ing, and Claire only hoped she didn't wake up disappointed one day. On the other hand, there were happy
couples here, like her aunt and uncle. Chaz was waving
at her and pointing to Jeremy. Jeremy was visibly
drooping, and when she suggested they both go up, he
didn't fuss.

The two of them held hands and walked up the steps,
and soon she had him tucked in bed. She stood at the top
of the stairs, digging for enough energy to go back
down, but the laughter trickling up clashed with her
pensiveness and, hoping she wouldn't be missed, she
moved quietly down the hall to her own room. With the
door shut behind her, all her emotions came swimming
up before her, teasing her tears and mocking the false
equilibrium she had shown the rest of the world for the
past weeks.

"Oh, Raleigh," she moaned softly. "Could it be I've
been wrong? Could it be you are somehow innocent?
But what about Sophie on the terrace, and what about
the handcuffs, and how could you have let so much time
go by without explaining it to me?" Hadn't he loved her
at all?

She sat on the edge of the bed, staring at her shoes and
wrapping her arms around herself against the cold that
was creeping into her soul. She loved him! Despite
everything, she loved him. And she ached to be with

him, wherever he was. She would never be ashamed of
how she'd trusted him with her heart and with her body.
Whatever he'd done, it didn't make the gift of her love
any less precious. The tears seeped under her lids and her
proud chin couldn't stay high any longer. What could
she do? What on earth was there to do? She walked to
the window and looked out on the empty street. An un-
controllable shiver ran through her. Outside, the city was
covered by swollen orange clouds, reluctant with spring
rain. She pulled the soft curtain against her cheek. She
hated missing him, and she hated feeling lonely, and
worst of all, a wicked little hope had been born from her
conversation with Jake. But it was useless. Even if Raleigh wasn't in jail, he was Sophie's; and even if he
wasn't Sophie's, he hadn't tried to reach her. No, he had
flown off to New York, letting her feel cheated and be-
reft. Her hopes plunged and blackness penetrated her
heart. If he didn't want her, well, she didn't want anything to do with him, either. So why couldn't she stop
crying?

Half-an-hour later, with a face hot and wet from
overdue tears, she sat up against her pillow and pulled
the quilt around her. She sniffed, and then laughed.

Well, at least I know I'm alive. I suppose this is all the
stuff the radio songs are made of, she thought. She
wiped her nose and flipped on the light next to her bed.
She had forgotten about Jolly's letter, and now it lay flat
and white on the bedside table. She stared at it uncertainly, and then reached out a hand to open it.

A card fell out onto her lap, and she picked it up in
disbelief. It was Raleigh Durban's business card, with his
Manhattan address and ''Photographer'' printed in the
corner. A boldly written note on the back read ''In case

of Claire's address,'' and there was a home phone number.

Claire's heart jolted against her ribs, and she grabbed for the letter.

Dear Claire,
Already we are missing you back here. Now that the excitement of the drug scandal is died down, we had to find something else to talk about. That's why I can tell you now that my daughter is going to get married to Jason Jr. Her father thinks she is too young, but they love each other and we were the same age, Juan and I. Imagine us all running around. Everybody is buying dates like crazy to help pay for the celebration. Come back at Easter time if you want to see it.

There is one other thing. Your friend Mr. Durban came by the day after you left and wanted your address. I told him I didn't have it because I don't like what he did, but maybe I was wrong. He gave me this card in case I changed my mind, and I will leave it up to you.

Take care of yourself, honey. Juan sends his love too.

Love, Jolly Avalos.

A crazy impulse jumped through her mind, sped along by the growing joy in her heart. He had tried to find her, after all, and he couldn't be in prison. She couldn't begin to understand it, and she wanted to find out more. The only way to do so was to talk to him, and here was the opportunity. She could call him.

Then came the thud. On the other hand, this card was ten days old. He could easily have found her by now if

he had persisted. Sophie had, Jake had and Earthquakes, Inc. could have helped him. She came soaring
down to a more rational plane and quelled the excitement that could yo-yo just as easily with despair. This
was going to take some thinking.

A soft knock pattered on the door, and Aunt Betty
leaned in her head. She was smiling, and she no longer
looked likely to fly. In fact, she looked a little shy.

"Are you asleep?" she asked unnecessarily.

Claire grinned, and patted the bed. Betty came in and
sat down, watching her closely and not missing the used
tissues distributed generously around the wastebasket.

"I'm sorry if I interrupted something earlier. We'd
had a few toasts."

"That's quite all right, Aunt Betty. Jake and I had just
been finishing up anyway."

She nodded, and looked down at her hands. Her
wedding ring shone dully on her stubby finger, and she
twisted it once. It had been a good anniversary, if her
general glow meant anything. Claire was glad for her.

"Did he say he was the one you knew in Death Valley?"

Claire knew what she meant.

"I did meet him there, but he hasn't caused me any
discomfort."

"I know you haven't wanted to talk about it," Betty
began, in a defensively loud voice. "But if you ever do,
I have lots of good advice for you. There's nothing we'd
like better than for you to be happy, Claire, and Chaz
and I have both realized by now that you have to do your
own picking, but we'd be glad to see you find someone
you care for, and if there's anything either one of us can
do for you, you know all you have to do is say so, and

we'll do whatever we can. Goodness, that was awk-ward. You know what I mean, though, don't you?''

Claire was touched.

"Thanks," she said simply.

Betty leaned over and gave her a hug, and Claire blinked rapidly.

"You're a brave, gallant, wonderful woman," she said. "Whoever he was, he's a fool and I wish I could give him a piece of my mind."

Claire chuckled into her shoulder.

"I wish you could too," she said, imagining the ex-change. "Really, I'm all right. Just give me a little time and I'll be fine."

Her aunt gave her a final hug and wished her good-night, feeling she'd done all she could. She shuffled off to her husband, no doubt to tell him all about it.

Exhausted, Claire listened to her receding steps, and without undressing, she rolled over, turned out the light and fell into deep, dreamless sleep.

## Chapter Eleven

Claire sat in her office. A letter from Earthquakes, Inc. had arrived that morning, approving her initial report and assuring her that any recommendations she might need would be more than glowing. It was what she had been hoping to hear, and it was one more string tied off. Finishing off her final report and checking her sources would be a matter of routine, and she would be looking at the completion. It was hard to believe, and already she was feeling a sense of letdown. All that work, winding down, and no one to celebrate with.

Before the dull pain could make her uselessly inactive, she plunged once again into her work, her fingers flying over the keys. A blast of lightning followed immediately by a tumble of thunder startled her almost out of her wits, and she looked up to see the rain streaming down her window. Would it never stop? All that water made her hands cold, and she was considering whether she really wanted another cup of coffee when Uncle Chaz came tapping on the door.

His face looked funny, and he studied her before he spoke.

"The man from Death Valley needs to talk to you. I left him in my office."

"I'll be right there," she said.

He nodded, and she thought he was going to add something else, but he walked heavily down the hall and off in the direction of the vending machines.

Claire was surprised, and not a little puzzled. What could Jake have to say that he hadn't said last night, and how had he convinced her uncle to give them his office? It was unheard of. With a sigh, she took a final glance at her work, turned off the machines and stood up. Her shoulders were tight from sitting the same way all morning, and she stretched before pulling the door toward her and stepping briskly into the hall. Her uncle's office was at the end of the hall. The big oak door was firmly closed, and a secretary was stationed before it at a desk.

"Hi, Kate. I think someone's waiting for me?"

Kate leaned back in her chair and looked her over, and then nodded.

"You might want to straighten your hair first," she said, looking sly.

Claire instinctively brushed it back from her face with her hand, and laughed. She reached for the door, speaking back over her shoulder.

"That won't be necessary."

But what she saw stopped her dead in her tracks. The door froze halfway closed, and Kate peeked curiously behind her.

Raleigh Durban turned slowly from his position at the window. His broad shoulders were clad in a deep-blue business suit, and a narrow aqua tie dropped from around his throat. His face was haggard, his eyes sleepless, but he was altogether stunning. He didn't say a word, and Claire, shaken to the roots of her being, barely managed to shut the door behind her. She was speechless, and her heart, when it started beating again, did so with jerky, irregular thuds.

"Claire," he began, moving around the desk toward her.

"Stop," she choked out. "What are you doing here?"

He paused, clenching his fist and taking a pace to one side.

"Claire, I don't know how to begin. There is a great deal I'd like to explain to you if you'll listen, but if you don't want to have me here, I'll leave."

She saw his jaw tighten, and noticed how pale he was. She stared at him, confused emotions making it impossible to construct a sentence. His eyes implored her to reply, and finally she moved forward into the room.

"I didn't expect to see you," she said, her voice flat and unencouraging. Inside, a fist was beating at her rib cage, trying to get out. She sat down, and gestured him to the chair opposite her. He took it, but almost immediately he stood again.

"This is ridiculous," he began. "I thought for three hours on the plane how I was going to do this, but now, seeing you, there's only one thing that seems important."

He spun back toward her, and pulled her ungently from her chair. She came breathlessly into his arms, while his eyes searched her own.

"Can it be I was wrong? I could have sworn on my life that I'd found a place in your heart, and I've been nearly insane trying to find you. Claire—" His voice was hardly a whisper. "Claire, how can I tell you? How can I begin—? Oh no. What have I said to make you cry?"

The tears had brimmed over her eyes and now ran unashamedly down her ashen cheeks. She felt rent in two, with both gladness and despair. He loved her. It showed all over him. And yet . . .

"Here, sit down," he said, guiding her back to the couch. "I knew I'd bungle it somehow. Here." He dug for his handkerchief and pushed it into her fist, then sat next to her and settled an arm around her shoulders. Once she had begun, the tears just came, big and silent, and his arm made it all the harder to stop.

"What is this?" she finally said. "I feel like some idiot fountain."

Raleigh momentarily withdrew, and she gave her nose a determined blow into the handkerchief. Now her eyes were hot, and her cheeks were flushed, and as she got control of herself, she realized he was sitting dangerously close. She still had a lot of questions to ask, even if she had lost all semblance of dignity. Even though the growing gladness she felt couldn't be quelled, she wasn't going to lose her head. That's where all the problems had started in the first place.

"I thought you were in jail." It seemed as good a place to start as any.

Raleigh took a breath and made his face serious, but his light eyes couldn't contain his happiness. Claire barely heard him, she was so distracted by those eyes.

"It's a long story, of course. For years, ever since my brother overdosed on some bad heroin, I've tried to do something about the dealer who sold him the stuff. That was Clem. While I was moving on with my photography, he was moving up in his world, too, and it was a long search tracking him down. I had to give up my photography for a while, when I started working for the feds. Well, the only way to catch him red-handed was to get into the game on the other side and then double-cross them. With my brother's history, it took less time than I expected to win their trust. My money had something to do with it, too, I suspect. Anyway, Mr. Ecks can verify the whole story, if you want to talk to him. He did some amazing work himself, and he had the patience sometimes, when I wanted to do something reckless. He never approved of getting you involved, by the way. We had to convince the locals I was aboveboard, and convince the dealers I was crooked, and any false turn would have tipped off either side that something was wrong.

"You seemed like the perfect solution; a companion already established and respected by the community. I was desperate enough to risk anybody, and once I realized what I'd done, it was too late. You were involved without knowing it. God, I'm glad to be out of it. The government was glad to have my help, and they offered me another assignment; but it's a horrible business. I didn't want to have anything more to do with it. Even so, they kept me busy with red tape for another week in New York, besides the tidying up in Death Valley. When you think of it, though, it's nothing to balance against all the lives Clem has destroyed, and I can finally be at rest about my brother. He never had a chance."

"But why couldn't you tell me? Why did you let me think you were as guilty as the rest of them?" She gulped back a new wave of tears as she remembered him cold and silent, a handcuffed criminal in the stark spotlight.

"If I had dreamed how much you knew, Claire, I would have told you the rest. But I was so afraid you would do something irregular and the dealers would suspect you were onto me. I could only trust that your ignorance would keep you safe. Then, when I found out they were shadowing you, I could have murdered them. My God, Claire. I figured it out that morning I left you at Salt Creek, all alone there in the rain. I hurried back and you were late and I didn't know where to look for you. It drove me crazy. Then you came waltzing up the boardwalk like nobody's business. It was all I could do not to grab you in my arms just at the sight of you."

She looked steadily into his face.

"But I did see something," she said. "I'd had the eeriest feeling, and then there was a flash up in the hills. I knew what it had to be, but I didn't know why."

A muscle tightened along his jaw, and his eyes darkened. He put a hand upon her cheek, touching her as if she were the most precious thing he'd ever known.

"I wish you had told me," he said quietly. "When I saw you on the playa, I knew you must have been torn with suspicions about me the whole time. If I had known, I would have dropped the whole thing."

She couldn't believe her ears, but there he was, saying each earnest word.

"These last days I've been in hell," he went on. "The satisfaction of finally grounding Clem meant nothing to me. Oh, Claire, you have no idea what I've been through."

"I think I do," she said softly. "For these ten days, I've been cursing your soul, hating you with an intensity that finally told me something. Why did it take you so long to come?"

A doleful smile crossed his face.

"You ask a mean question," he said. "I could tell you the government kept me busy, and it's true that I wasn't going to come look for you until I was absolutely sure it would be safe; but in all, that took only four or five days. Then I could tell you you're hard to trace, and that's true also. I asked around, but your friends all had some reason for not giving me your address." A wry twist touched his lips. "I learned from Jolly in particular that I was a lout. Let's see. I think it was 'a lout and a cheat and a no-good pestering get-out-of-here *cucaracha*.' That seems to have been the opinion in general.

"Then I tried Earthquakes, Inc. Harris must have been expecting my call, for he told his secretary that he was unavailable, and that you had asked them not to give out your address. I was back in at work by then, and the gallery was harassing me to produce the show they thought I'd been working on. I spent my days in the lab, developing and printing until my eyes stung from focusing. I could honestly tell you I've been too busy.

"But Claire, to be really honest, I didn't want to come. I was haunted by your face, by your eyes trusting me and demanding honesty from me. I knew how damning that arrest must have looked, and I was too proud. I didn't think I could ask you to forgive me. I didn't think you would ever be able to trust me again, and I couldn't bear that. I decided you were better off without me, and then I blocked you out. I gave up. I worked like crazy, afraid to sleep because of my dreams. I pretended I was interested in your portrait for purely aesthetic reasons, but I came back to it constantly. Inside I was crumbling."

He stopped for a moment.

"Is it wrong to tell you this?" he asked uncertainly, his color heightened, and his eyes watching her keenly.

"No," she said gently. "I want to hear."

"Then I met a friend of yours, or rather, she met me. I'd contributed a dozen photos to the gallery show, and by some fluke, or miracle, this college friend of yours came to the opening. She recognized you in one of my pieces, and asked me how I knew you. I nearly keeled over right there. I realized I'd been fooling myself, trying to convince myself I didn't care. Here she was babbling about something you'd done to her at school and all I could think was: I had to explain. I had to see you, and see if there was a chance. I'm afraid I was so excited to get your address, I didn't get her name. I left the show right then. That was last night. I came as fast as I could."

That sounded pretty good to her. Her curiosity was piqued.

"But, when did you take a picture of me?"

"That morning at Dante's View. You stepped over to the cliff ahead of me, and I took it then. I hardly even knew you then, but my camera did. It's a wonderful portrait. A profile. I'll give it to you."

She smiled, pleased by the idea. It would be great to see his work, and she was honored to hold a place in it. He touched the corner of her mouth.

"That smile. You are the most beautiful woman, Claire. Again and again I found myself watching you, just watching the way you moved, wondering when you'd be likely to turn around and give me one of those smiles." He chuckled low in his throat. "You were just as likely to turn around and bite my head off."

She gasped.

"Oh, Claire," he laughed. "My precious, gullible Claire. The desert magic can't be accountable for what happens in Chicago, can it? No, I'm afraid we'll have to make do with what we've got. That shouldn't be too bad.''

She drank in every word, longing to believe him, yet hesitating. There was still something bothering her, and she didn't know how to ask it.

"What is it?" he asked gently. "If there's something else I've done . . ." He left it hanging, and she knew she shouldn't be afraid to ask.

"What about Sophie?"

His expression didn't change at all, and then he lifted an eyebrow.

"Sophie? What about her?"

Was he serious? He must be. This was going to be awkward. She inhaled and began again.

"That last day, in the hotel, I saw you kiss her. Believe me, I didn't want to, but I did. And then she sent Jake to ask me about you." She couldn't say any more.

He was stumped, and then, to her amazement, he began to chuckle.

"Jake here? Wouldn't that be just like her? Oh, Claire, Sophie and I have been friends for years. Periodically she tries to convince me we're more than friends, and I let her try, but each time we come back to the same conclusion. We'd never suit, and we both know it.''

Claire wasn't so sure.

"Then that day?"

"We had just reached the conclusion. I was thanking her for letting me intrude on her party of guests, and she was agreeing once again we'd go our own ways. I was still so angry at you about Harris. I guess I didn't care if you misinterpreted what you saw. In fact, I was almost glad that I might be able to hurt you, though I'm not proud of it. I knew you'd be safer if you weren't involved with me anymore anyway." He thought for a second. "I don't think we kissed," he said, half to himself.

The image of the shadows emerged again in her mind's eye, and she quickly realized she could have misread it. She suspected, however, that Raleigh didn't know quite all of what went on with Sophie, for those wicked green eyes belonged to more than just a friend. Well, it wasn't up to Claire to undeceive him. Besides, her heart was lifting with every explanation he was making.

"Satisfied?"

Claire became conscious of how close he had come, and she blushed, looking unabashedly into his face.

"That's the worst of it, isn't it?" she agreed.

He leaned back on the couch ever so casually. Then he looked at her, grinning, and the light of a different appreciation crowded the humor out of his eyes. She was drawn to him as surely as by a magical thread of energy, and sliding comfortably into his arms was as natural as breathing.

"God, how I've wanted you," he whispered hoarsely. A kiss went burning through her senses as she wrapped her arms around his shoulders and nestled against him. "Claire," he said, an endearing catch in his voice, "you know I love you, don't you?"

She nodded, and her own feelings were clear. For several minutes, conversation was suspended as they hungrily explored their newfound closeness. He hadn't shaved, and she had a smudge of ink under her chin, but neither seemed to mind. Suddenly she was struck by the humor of it.

"I've never necked in my uncle's office before."

He chuckled.

"I don't think he'd mind."

"I suppose not," she said.

His caress trailed down her hip, and she boldly copied the gesture.

"I always thought you were a bit of a prude."

"That's just because I haven't had the proper opportunities," she retorted.

His hands stopped and he smiled into her impish face.

"No time like the present," he said devilishly.

She didn't get the chance to disagree, even if she had wanted to. His kiss was intoxicating, and his nearness was heady with his warm, masculine scent. His eyes opened to smile at her, and her own eyes grew soft and heavy-lidded with desire. His powerful hands cradled her against him as they stretched out on the couch. Then she heard one of his shoes hit the floor, and she nearly laughed with pleasure. Her pulse throbbed with his lightest touch, and she responded ardently. What paradise it was to be able to love him freely, with no more reservations. For a time Claire forgot everything, lost in the tremulous happiness of complete love, and when she surfaced, it was with the realization that this was only the beginning. He rolled lazily on his side, regarding her earnestly and smoothing the hair back from her forehead. She watched the shadows shift on his face, and wondered how she had ever mistrusted him.

"That night on the playa, I didn't know how I was ever going to explain it all to you, and I was so scared for your safety. I couldn't believe Ecks let you come. He figured you knew everything, but even so, it was incredibly foolhardy." He smiled. "But then, I'm forgetting you had him wrapped around your finger. Him, poor Jake, that Dell person. How many other guys did you have ready to drive you around, or whatever else you wanted? It drove me crazy."

"But Raleigh, they were all nothing, compared to you. You must have known that."

"Well, of course I thought so, but I didn't know then that you're as smart as you are."

She smiled, looking in his dear, handsome face.

"I suppose I should ask you to marry me," he said at last.

She chuckled, putting a hand to his tanned cheek.

"Cocky kind of guy, aren't you?"

He grinned and pulled her close.

"I knew from that first time I heard your sassy voice yelling from that ridiculous car that this was an unusual woman. Then I couldn't see you often enough. That day in Shoshone. I wanted to touch you so badly. You were so incredibly pretty, and you were shopping in Shoshone, of all places. I got you so mad." He laughed, remembering. "You'll have to watch my temper, Claire. You threw me that bait, and I grabbed it, and to be honest, kissing you was one of the most thorough pleasures I'd had in a long time. I could have driven off to Las Vegas and married you right then, without knowing a thing more about you. I knew I'd gone too far, though, when you wound up to hit me."

"It was either that or faint dead away. Oh, Raleigh. If only we'd been talking to each other the whole time. Think of all the confusion we'd have avoided. It's almost funny how..."

He settled her close against his chest and brushed her forehead with his lips.

"I almost can't believe we managed to get together myself. I hated lying to you. I hated it, that night, when you asked me point-blank, and I was too stupid to realize I should tell you everything. God, how you looked at me." His lips twisted in an instant of self-mockery, and then he laughed. His tone lightened. "I don't know about you, but I don't intend to be keeping any more secrets. I'll tell you bluntly anything you want to know about my very legal photography studio. In fact, I hope you'll contribute to it. What's so funny?"

She was chuckling into his collar.

"I like that. 'You don't know about me.' It's a relief, too, because I wasn't sure how I'd keep my secrets from you, but since you don't mind . . ."

"What secrets?" he demanded.

She only laughed more until he had to kiss her to protect her from going into fits.

"You won't have to try," he said finally. "You'll always intrigue me anyway, even without secrets. Little runt. How can you make me laugh so much?"

"It's your age," she said confidentially. "I do have a secret by the way. Remember Jolly?"

He rolled his eyes. Did he remember Jolly!

"Yes, well, she has a daughter who's going to get married to Jason Jr. Remember him from Shoshone? No. Well, it doesn't matter. They're getting married and Jolly invited me back for the wedding."

"So you're going back?"

"Well, I never did get to have dinner on the terrace of the hotel like I wanted to."

"Don't tell me you miss your trailer, too. You couldn't possibly have been fond of that little box. I'll have you know we are living in a regular place, with a regular-size kitchen, and Raleigh's Desert Delight will be a staple, right alongside the milk and eggs."

She chuckled, remembering that evening.

"Harris was such a jerk, wasn't he?"

"What did you ever do with him? I nearly strangled him that night," he said conversationally.

"Oh, he succumbed to my charms. I just sent him off." She had determined to forget about that wretched breakfast meeting.

Raleigh was mumbling something about her charms and trying to retuck her hair behind her ear to keep it out of the way.

"What was that?" she asked.

"Just that I hope you won't feel compelled to charm absolutely every man you meet. It would keep us awfully busy bumping them off, one after the other."

She smiled up at him, drawing him close with all the charm at her disposal.

"I think we'll have better things to do," she said, and did one of them.

# Take 4 Silhouette Romance novels
# FREE

Then preview 6 brand-new Silhouette Romance® novels—delivered to your door as soon as they are published—for 15 days without obligation. When you decide to keep them, pay just $1.95 each, *with no shipping, handling or other charges of any kind!*

Each month, you'll meet lively young heroines and share in their thrilling escapades, trials and triumphs...virile men you'll find as attractive and irresistible as the heroines do...and colorful supporting characters you'll feel you've always known.

Start with 4 Silhouette Romance novels absolutely FREE. They're yours to keep without obligation, and you can cancel at any time.

As an added bonus, you'll also get the Silhouette Books Newsletter FREE with every shipment. Every issue is filled with news on upcoming books, interviews with your favorite authors, even their favorite recipes.

Simply fill out and return the coupon today!
*This offer is not available in Canada.*

## *Silhouette* ❦ *Romance*®

**Silhouette Books, 120 Brighton Rd., P.O. Box 5084, Clifton, NJ 07015-5084**

---

**Clip and mail to: Silhouette Books,**
**120 Brighton Road, P.O. Box 5084, Clifton, NJ 07015-5084**

YES. Please send me 4 Silhouette Romance novels FREE. Unless you hear from me after I receive them, send me six new Silhouette Romance novels to preview each month as soon as they are published. I understand you will bill me just $1.95 each (a total of $11.70) with no shipping, handling, or other charges of any kind. There is no minimum number of books that I must buy, and I can cancel at any time. The first 4 books are mine to keep.　　**BR18L6**

Name _____ (please print)

Address _____ Apt. #

City _____ State _____ Zip

Terms and prices subject to change. Not available in Canada.
SILHOUETTE ROMANCE is a service mark and registered trademark.　　SR-SUB-1

**Available July 1986**

# Silhouette Desire

# Texas Gold

The first in a great new
Desire trilogy by Joan Hohl.

In *Texas Gold* you can meet the
Sharp family—twins Thackery
and Zackery.

With Thackery, Barbara Holcomb,
New York model, embarks on an
adventure, as together they search for a
cache of stolen gold. For Barbara and
Thack, their gold is discovered in the
bright, rich vein of their love.

Then get to know Zackery and his half
sister Kit in *California Copper* and
*Nevada Silver*—coming soon from
Silhouette Books.

# *Silhouette Romance*

# COMING NEXT MONTH

**THE GLORIOUS QUEST—Rita Rainville**
When Kelly's mother and Jase's father ran off together, their
children chased after them, determined to bring them to their
senses—and promptly fell in love.

**JURY OF HIS PEERS—Debbie Macomber**
Wholesome, sincere Ted had always gotten on Caroline's nerves.
When they were both called for jury duty, temperatures in the
courtroom rose—and not from the court case!

**SOMETHING SENTIMENTAL—Mia Maxam**
Mallory was happy with her job as general manager of a small,
homey FM radio station—until the station was sold. Now she had
to contend with the new boss, Keith Alexander.

**SWEPT AWAY—Donna McDowell**
Jarod was everything Amanda wanted in a man, but he belonged
to another woman. Refusing to come between them, Amanda
tried to forget Jarod. But she had been swept away....

**WHERE THERE'S A WILL—Joan Smith**
Kathryn didn't mind when Joshua dragged her into a situation
straight out of a bad mystery novel. But when a man was as
dangerously handsome as Joshua, he could drag her anywhere!

**GOOD TIME MAN—Emilie Richards**
Jessica had dreamed of Alex Granger's kisses since she was
sixteen. But four years away at school hadn't prepared her for his
kind of loving—or leaving.

## AVAILABLE THIS MONTH

**UNHEAVENLY ANGEL**
Annette Broadrick

**MAGIC CITY**
Lynnette Morland

**AN IRRITATING MAN**
Lass Small

**MIRAGE**
Mary O'Caragh

**THE RIGHT MOVES**
Arlene James

**AMENDED DREAMS**
Glenda Sands